Lin Bird lives in the South Wales valleys and was a teacher until a diagnosis of leukaemia and a bone marrow transplant led to early ill-health retirement. Dealing with a life changing illness brought a sharper focus on the things that matter in life. Writing had always been a guilty pleasure but it was the imposition of the lockdown in March 2020 that created a space to bring her writing to the forefront. Lin picked up the threads of a novel that had been bubbling away on the back burner of her mind for many years. Believing in the life changing nature of reading and the importance of redemptive acts led to the writing of *The Lift Book Club*.

For Diane, who has always believed in me.

Lin Bird

The Lift Book Club

AUSTIN MACAULEY PUBLISHERS™

LONDON • CAMBRIDGE • NEW YORK • SHARJAH

A CIP catalogue record for this title is available from the British Library.

ISBN 9781398439276 (Paperback)
ISBN 9781398439283 (ePub e-book)

www.austinmacauley.com

First Published 2022
Austin Macauley Publishers Ltd®
1 Canada Square
Canary Wharf
London
E14 5AA

Thank you to Diane Walker, Marion Porter and Dinnella Shelton who were invaluable first critics. Also thanks goes to the team of Austin Macauley Publishers for believing in this book and bringing it to publication.

Prologue

Gabe looked around him. This must be the right place. He entered through the glass doors. He hadn't realised until he stepped in, how cold and hard the outside had been. He stepped up to the reception desk. A chap in some kind of uniform stood holding a clipboard. It seemed to Gabe that he was the stereotype of the 'jobs worth' with his uniform and papers. Flicking through, as though he hadn't seen Gabe approach.

Gabe cleared his throat, and for a second thought, he was going to continue to be ignored but the man looked up. A question in his stare. "Gabe Somerset, I was told to come here."

The man looked down at his clipboard and made a great production of running his pen up and down the page, as though unable to find Gabe's name. Then the movement stopped and the man looked up. "Oh, not being sent down." He sounded disappointed. "Through there." He indicated a long featureless corridor that stretched away from the desk.

Gabe began to walk. His footsteps created a muffled echo and the overhead lighting made the corridor feel unreal. He was reminded of the time his dad had to take him to hospital in the middle of the night, well 10 o'clock. He had fallen out of bed. Or that's what he'd told his parents. In reality, he had been bouncing on the bed as if it were a trampoline. His arm had hurt and he remembered Mum creating a sling with one of her scarves. All night he could smell that reassuring scent that was his mum. The doctor had thought he had broken his arm and so his dad had to take him to have an X-ray. His dad took him in a wheelchair down a corridor just like this one. And he remembered that his dad had tried to cheer him up by running and swerving along the corridor. He still remembered that sickening mix of fear and excitement.

Another desk grew into focus. This time a young woman was sat and smiled as he approached. "Gabe Somerset?"

"Yes."

"Mr Bonhom is expecting you. If you'd like to take the middle door," she pointed.

Gabe felt worse than when he went to the last meeting with his boss and knew he was going to get fired. Not that he blamed him. He had a business to run and that meant reliable, sober and prompt employees. Gabe had ceased to be such an ideal worker.

He drew in a deep breath and knocked on the door. He heard a rumbling bass, "Come in."

Gabe entered and saw a neatly dressed man of about sixty. He was wearing a smart, dark suit with a collar and tie. His hair was grey with white at the temples. He seemed tall even sat down. When he stood he was a giant of a man. "Ah, Gabe? May I call you Gabe? I've read your file and I feel like I have known you forever."

Gabe held his hand out and shook the proffered paw. "Yes, sir."

"No 'sirs' here, my boy. I am Michael or even Mike if you prefer. Now I've looked through your file and the powers that be," he paused, "have decided that you are not a bad young man but that in the last few years you have made some very silly choices."

Gabe hung his head. Memories of drug-taking and stealing to fund his habit played. He'd lost his job and the drugs had been a get out. They'd made life more bearable but, of course, then they'd been the reason for the other bad choices he'd made. A wave of misery broke over him and tears escaped. He surreptitiously wiped them away. He couldn't bring himself to look at Michael. He'd been an idiot. A selfish bloody idiot. He deserved everything that was coming his way. He mentally shook himself and sat up straighter. He looked Michael in the eye.

There was no condemnation there. There was gentle understanding. "You know you have to make amends, don't you Gabe?"

Gabe nodded. How? He didn't have a clue.

Michael leant back in his chair, it creaked ominously. "We are going to set you up in a place called Swanton. It's nowhere near where you're from so you're not going to run into any old 'friends'."

Gabe heard the quotation marks.

"This is a new approach. Normally you would be given some form of community work for set hours."

Gabe nodded. That's what he had been expecting.

"But we're not sure that actually allows the culprit, I hope you don't mind my use of that word?"

Gabe shook his head.

"That allows the culprit not to think. Do this work and I'm done. No real thought process about making things right, or at least better. So," he paused again, "you will have a job as a lift operator in a small block of flats. There are six flats and each resident has his or her burden. We are asking you to make their lives better."

Gabe panicked. "But how can I do that?"

"I don't know, Gabe. That's for you to decide," Michael held Gabe's stare.

This was not what Gabe had been expecting. Nothing in his past experience had prepared him for this. How was he supposed to interact with strangers? He was useless with strangers. And how could he, an ex-junkie and petty thief possibly have anything to offer ordinary, law-abiding people?

"We have organised a room in the local Half Way House and you will have a weekly spending allowance. If, for any reason, you need more you will need to contact me."

"But…but…" Gabe was lost for words.

"The manager of the Hostel is a woman called Pat, she will take you to the job on your first day and she will get a message to me if you tell her you want to speak with me."

Michael stood and held out his hand. "We have every faith in you, Gabe. Now you need to have faith in yourself. Pat should be waiting outside to take you to your new home and career."

Mutely Gabe stood and shook hands. Michael added, "You may find it helpful to write about the choices you made in the past. It may help you to reflect on what went wrong."

Gabe nodded as he turned to leave. He looked back over his shoulder and his last memory was of Michael smiling and seeming to give him a blessing.

Diary... Memoir of an Idiot

I've decided this is a memoir, not a diary. Michael suggested I needed to reflect on what I've done. Where to start? When I try to work out where it all went wrong I keep linking back even further. I think I'll start at the beginning, the beginning of my life and work forward.

I was born to Dave and Carol Somerset in a tiny bedsit. Dave was a labourer on building sites and Carol was only just out of school. My earliest memory is of moving to the flat in Shakespeare House. We were on the fourth floor and had to use the lift. I think I was about three, maybe four, but I'd never been in a lift before. I still remember the sinking feeling in my tummy as it started to rise. I loved it. Every opportunity I got I wanted to ride the lift.

I had a happy childhood until Dad died. I was eight. He had been unwell for a while. I can't really remember it but one minute he was there, feeling, 'a bit crook' and then he was gone. When I was older, Mum explained it was pancreatic cancer and it had all happened very quickly. I hadn't been aware of how tight money was until Dad died. Then it seemed to be the only thing Mum talked about. She ended up getting two jobs; cleaning the local school in the evening and a block of offices in town first thing in the morning.

I'd always had a lot to do with Gran Somerset, there was no Grandpa and Mum's family had sort of disowned her when she met and married Dad. Gran lived in the same block of flats as us, but on the second floor. She'd take me out for afternoons to give my mum a chance to do stuff when Dad was still alive. And when he died she had more to do. She'd arrive at our flat just before six as Mum was going off to work and she'd make sure I had breakfast and was clean and tidy to go to school. In the evening, I went to her flat and she gave me tea and helped with homework if I had any. I really enjoyed reading to her. I loved books. I loved the time with Gran.

Then, when I went to secondary school, Mum decided that she was going to do night classes to get some qualifications. She said she'd wasted her time at school and she wanted to improve herself. She was always on at me to make the most of school and not have to go back. Part of me was quite blasé and didn't really take it on board but, I think, somewhere in my subconscious, I could see how hard it was for her; going back and doing at twenty-something all the stuff she should have done in her teens.

Mum doing classes meant I spent more time with Gran. Not just the nights Mum was out but also at the weekends because Mum needed time to do her homework, as she said. I suppose I could have been put out, being off-loaded onto Gran but I wasn't. Time with Gran was great; whether we stopped in and played cards, read together or watched old films; or if we went out to the local park and had ice cream on the way back. I loved it.

So where did things go wrong?

Chapter 1

No one knew when Gabe arrived in the lift at Harrington Hall: it seemed there was a time before Gabe and a time after Gabe: but nobody could pinpoint when the change occurred. Perhaps Miss Ilene James, the eldest tenant, could have shed some light, but her grip on time was as light as a feather's touch.

First, there was just Gabe. The tenants of Harrington Hall left their respective flats one Monday morning and found Gabe in place at the lift's controls. He greeted each of them pleasantly and wished them a good day as they left. Although dressed only in cotton trousers and a white shirt he made it appear as though he was in livery.

By Friday of that first week, he greeted each tenant by name and each found the lift waiting for them as they left their flat, as though the mere thought of their need to leave had communicated itself to the lift. Only Miss James was elusive. Being a lady of a certain age, and a little fey, her life had little routine. However, in time, Gabe deduced there was a method in her perambulations; mainly to do with which way the wind was blowing.

Then there was Gabe and a Persian rug. Slightly worn in places, with the fringe displaying bald patches, but nevertheless a Persian Rug. Its dusty blues and reds, echoes of its once Victorian grandeur. The more observant passenger may have discerned that the rug was a little long for the space and the end had been folded neatly to square it off. A small coconut matting had been placed centrally on the rug, just at the point where one entered the lift and passengers felt compelled to wipe their feet before proceeding further into the lift. A smile of appreciation from Gabe cheered them as they travelled up and down.

Next came the leather, fireside chair. Its rusted skin cracked and rubbed raw along the armrests. A few of the deep creases in the back's harlequin design were missing their brass studs. Yet it still managed to convey that it had once been a very fine chair and should be accorded the respect of that fact. Miss James viewed it suspiciously on first seeing it, but the slow descent and ascent from her third floor, single bedroom flat encouraged her to perch cautiously on the edge. In time, she relaxed into its curves.

Mrs Cole and Mrs Davies, both on the second floor, two-bedroom flats, gratefully set bags of shopping in its deep seat; pleased to take the weight of their scored fingers. Jennifer Davies, four and three-quarter years old, would climb up eagerly and sit with straight legs out proudly in front of her.

As though sensing the loneliness of a single, fireside chair, a second chair appeared. Somewhat a poorer relative from the country, this one was a wooden captain's chair so loved by schoolmasters of old. In an attempt to blend with the other furnishings, a fusty cushion of red velvet, worn smooth, sat primly on the seat. This item seemed to appeal less to the passengers and was only used by Gabe himself when the lift was empty.

The final piece to complete the lift's décor was a little half-moon, pie crust table. Woodworms had once banqueted on its fine, barley twist legs and heavy boots had scuffed the brass protectors on its feet. The table surface, however, had a fine shine and a little lace doily covered its immodest glow. No one remarked on these additions but all, if only subconsciously, felt the nomadic room was better than the cavernous freight lift; a reminder of the industrial past of Harrington Hall.

Memoir of an Idiot

The job has started. The lift is enormous! Apparently, according to Pat, who took me there on my first day, the building used to be a factory, she thought ceramics but wasn't sure. Swanton was famous in the nineteenth century for its ceramics. Anyway, for some reason, the developer decided to leave the freight lift in situ. I must admit I felt quite cowed, just me in this vast space but I've done something about it. I've turned it into a mini room. There's a house conversion going on a few streets away and they've been turfing out all the old stuff into a skip. I did ask one of the chaps first and he said I was welcome to anything I could use, so I found an old rug. You know, one of those woven ones from somewhere like Persia: a Persian rug. There was also a really scrappy leather chair. I wasn't sure how I was going to get it to Harrington Hall but one of the chaps said he'd give me a lift in his van. It was on his way apparently. I thought that was really kind of him. He doesn't know me from Adam.

A few days later I noticed a wooden chair and a little table. I liked the table it reminded me of my Gran's flat. She had wooden furniture with twisted legs and everything with a lovely glow from all the polishing. She let me help sometimes so when I borrowed some polish and a cloth from Pat and cleaned up the two items, I could only think of Gran.

I think I've met all of the residents so I know which floors they want when they return, but not sure of all their names yet. No one's mentioned the rug or the chairs yet. They just seem to have accepted them. I think it makes the lift more homely and having chairs is good for me, I can sit and read because there is an awful lot of downtime.

Things at home went on in the same pattern for years. Mum got her qualifications and then was able to get better-paid jobs with more reasonable hours. She then decided she liked this learning stuff and managed to save money to join the Open University. She always maintained that studying 'Educating Rita' gave her the idea of keeping on with learning.

I was also doing all right with school. I'm no brainbox but I found I liked Design, especially the electrical side of it and that made me work harder in Maths because I could see the sense in it. Just before the end of year 11, my Design teacher suggested I should look at trying for an apprenticeship in one of the local firms. I did and got one. Stephens Electrical Engineering. Mr Bradey was my boss. He was all right. He checked that I was going to college once a week and what assignments I had to do. Looking back I can see that I really landed on my feet there. The older chaps were good fun and would make suggestions about how I could improve on something, or even once, thanking me for showing one of them how to use the computer-aided design package the firm had just introduced.

Life was good. I still spent time with Gran but more of it was spent hanging around with my mates or the occasional girlfriend. I didn't have many girlfriends, I was too shy to chat them up and I had bad acne, which really bumps your confidence down.

Chapter 2

Gabe got to know each resident via their washing habits: or more precisely their laundry habits. Interestingly, Miss James was the most regular. Despite appearing as though she and the world had but a distant acquaintanceship, she did her laundry every Monday morning just after nine. Gabe would bring the lift and she would balance her little washing basket on the seat of her three-wheeled walker and get on. In time, rather than go back to her flat she would come and sit in the lift with Gabe.

"Monday was always wash day in my childhood," she explained. "And it would take all day. None of this pop it in a machine and walk away. My mum had one of those hot tubs and a mangle when I was very small. But it would take all morning. If you were lucky you got it dry on the same day but in the wetter months, you had washing hanging from the scullery ceiling and on a clothes horse in the back room. It was the only room that had constant heat because the little stove heated the water.

"I remember, about an hour before my dad was due home, one of us would stoke the stove to heat the water for his home wash. First thing he did when he got home was to strip to his vest and trousers, braces swinging at his hips and he would have a wash at the sink." She laughed. "I've never known anyone to splash water around like he did. You'd think he was wrestling fish in that sink!"

Some days she also brought a thermos flask and they would sit and drink sweet tea whilst Miss James drifted with her memories. She frequently spoke of her days as personal assistants to a number of businessmen in a range of trades.

"I grew up in Swanton and got my first secretarial job here, but I moved around a lot, following job opportunities. I've lived in umpteen different towns and cities of the North but I was happy to retire back here twenty years ago. I still had friends here then, not so much family. I had a sister but she and her husband emigrated to Canada. I did go across to see her a couple of times. They had two girls but once Enid died I lost touch. Now my friends are either in the cemetery or lost in their own minds," she sighed heavily and then shook herself. "But mustn't grumble. I've still got my health and I get about."

On one occasion she reminisced about her trips abroad. "Mr Frank Byford, sanitary ware, that's toilets and sinks to you and me. Oh, he was an ambitious man. When he heard that the Berlin wall was being torn down he got us on a plane the next day. I think we were one of the first, maybe even, the first, western, non-German business to go across into East Berlin. It was grim. I don't mind telling you. I was more than a little afraid, but Frank went straight to the hotels and talked with the managers. Selling them tales of gleaming modern sanitary wares for their highly discerning western visitors who would be flocking to their doors. He really could sell snow to the Eskimos!"

The Captain, Captain Roger Clive formerly of the Merchant Navy, was equally regular in his laundry habits. Friday morning was his preferred time. "Wash on Friday. Air overnight. Ironing Saturday. I like to listen to Radio 4." He was a lot less forthcoming than Miss James. Occasional, less guarded moments led Gabe to believe that he too had no family, "Time at sea leaves little time for life on land," he once pronounced. Gabe knew he spent time at The Old Comrades Club. It was a weekly occurrence, although the Captain tended to only go once a month. He was never explicit in whether he met friends or mere acquaintances there, but he was always immaculately turned out and returned at the same time after each gathering.

He too began to spend time with Gabe rather than returning to his flat whilst his washing swirled and tumbled, his talk was of the state of the world. He went out most days and invariably came back with an armful of papers. "Got to keep up with the world. Don't know what they'll try and get away with."

Although not your regular conspiracy theorist he did have his pet hobby horse: the murder of JFK. "Inside job. That's my theory. Too liberal for the money men." He also seemed to read a lot, and not just about JFK. Once a week, normally a Tuesday he would take a walk to the local library, off the High Street. He carried his books in a smart blue rucksack. "Much easier to carry weight on your back." And weight it must have been, Gabe concluded, seeing the way it bulged.

Sam, the third resident on the floor with Miss James and the Captain, was far more haphazard in his laundry visits. Part of that was to do with his shift patterns, Gabe was sure, but part was down to a young man living alone. Once Sam got to know Gabe a little, and how amenable he was, he would often throw his washing into a machine and ask Gabe to chuck it into the tumble dryer once it was finished. Gabe was more than happy to do this and often went a step further and folded the clothes from the tumble dryer, presenting Sam with a tidy pile of folded, clean washing at the end of his shift.

On the rare occasions when Sam was home for his washing load, he would sit with Gabe and they would pleasantly chat about Swanton and what it was like being a stranger in the town. "With my shift patterns I don't get much of a chance to socialise outside of the hospital," Sam once remarked. "You're not supposed to have romantic liaisons at work, but when your shift patterns and the pressure of work only allow you time off with the same people you work with, it's not really surprising if some romances blossom, is it?"

Sam's other commitment was to exercise. He regularly ran to and from the hospital and was a member of the local council sports centre. "Not looking to get a muscle-bound body, but I do find exercise stimulates my endorphins. Running home from a really stressful shift is a great way of unwinding, especially as nine times out of ten I need to sleep once I've eaten."

Chapter 3

The second-floor residents, Mrs Davies and Mrs Cole were less methodical in their laundry visits. Mrs Cole was happy to sit and talk with Gabe on some occasions. She was quite outward going and Gabe found it easy to sit and talk with her or sit quietly with few words. She had been a teacher at the large secondary school on the other side of Swanton. "It has quite a mixed catchment, really. We have the Swanton lot, but they are a mix of the estate kids and the suburban ones, and then of course, there's the rural intake." She laughed. "They all think they're so worldly wise but put them in one of their peers' environments and they'd be lost."

She'd retired a few years ago, "Partly burn out, I think. I taught History. When I started teaching we went through chronologically, so kids had some idea of what went before. But with the National Curriculum, you jump about all over the place. I know the Tudors and Stuarts are important and that the Victorian era was the bedrock of a lot of our social and economic understandings today, but other periods are just as important. Magna Carta. The Hanoverians," she paused, "Sorry, on my soapbox."

Gabe could tell that she was passionate about teaching. "I got out because I knew I'd run out of energy. I know the general public moan about our nine to three hours and our holiday time, but honestly, hand on heart I can say that on average I worked a sixty-hour week, most weeks in term time. And every holiday is finishing the marking and recording of the last term and preparing lessons for the coming term. Do you know, I remember once, we'd gone out for a nice meal and there was a crowd in there? You know the type: raised voices, thinking everyone wanted to hear the important things they were saying." A lip curled in disdain. "And this one woman was lamenting the non-show of one of their tribe, she said: 'She told me she had lesson plans to prepare. I said, surely this is your second year of teaching can't you use last years!'"

She took a deep breath, the memory still having the power to raise strong emotion. "And that's the problem. People don't understand that every year, every lesson has to be tailored to the individuals in that group. I may have the resources I need to use, but I still have to work out which ways to present them: will Julie need a larger text? Would some of them benefit from their own copy that they can write around? Will this class work better as individuals or in little teams? You're constantly having to fiddle and alter the way you do things." She sat back as though exhausted. "And then there is the record-keeping and marking. Every piece of work having to have levels ascribed, every teacher's comment having to point out what was missing and what they need to target to get to the next level. Trying to do a balancing act between affirming the child's endeavours and fulfilling government prescriptions. I just got tired. I think teaching is a young person's game, except that very few of them have the experience to be a good disciplinarian. Sorry, Gabe. Even though I've been out of teaching a good few years now, it still is something I am passionate about."

"I admire that passion. I'm sure your past pupils were lucky to have you as their teacher."

Mrs Davies was less forthcoming than Mrs Cole. She frequently disappeared back to her flat when she had put a load of washing in. Gabe assumed that being a working Mum and having a four-year-old to chase after, time was too precious to sit and chat. On a few, a very few, occasions she did stop and chat. Her conversation was then mainly about Jenny and the mischief that little ones can unintentionally get into.

"We found this really old video and John got it formatted to a DVD and it's Paul McCartney's *Frog Chorus*. Do you know it?"

Gabe shook his head.

"It was in the charts years ago, the 1990s, I think. Anyway, the chorus of the song has the frogs singing, 'Bom, bom, bom, ieiah!' Well, Jenny has got it into her head that frogs are called Bombom ieiahs!"

Another time it was, "I had to stop and talk to Jenny's teacher yesterday. Apparently, there were some boys being naughty so Jenny went up to them and told them if they didn't stop she would have to put them outside. I think they were so surprised that they did quieten down, but soon were being silly again, so," and here Mrs Earniston grinned, "I know I shouldn't be smiling but this just seems so funny. "She went and got their coats, told them to put them on and stood them outside the classroom door. And they did what she told them to! The teacher was trying not to smile when she told me because Jenny was there. So we had a serious conversation about what children can do and what teachers are allowed to do. But her teacher winked as we left."

Mrs Davies was also very proud of her husband's achievements. "He was headhunted for this post, you know? He'd never dreamt of moving on from his first post. He was happy and good at what he did, but he never did understand just how good that was. Not until they approached him directly." She shook her head in wonderment. "He's not a vain man. Just does his best," she sighed contentedly.

The only person Gabe didn't get to know better through the laundry was Mrs White in number one, on the ground floor. She had no need for a sit down in the lift whilst her washing spun. There were a few times when she had taken her son, Robbie, to the third floor. Partly because he wanted to ride in the lift and partly because he liked to look at the views from the top of the building.

Alison's Story

She'd always been a studious girl, leaving college with three 'A' levels, but her mum didn't want her going to university. "Go out and earn your keep," she'd said. She would have liked to go on but was worried about the amount of debt she would create, so she opted for a job. It was a good job in an accountancy firm and they were prepared to pay for her to study to get the appropriate qualifications. It meant she would be there for at least six years, but that was job security.

All those plans. Life sorted. Then came the college party, just before the autumn term. Everyone came; those going off to uni, those staying on another year and those, like herself, off into the world of work. It was a good night. The pub they were in was happy to have the music loud and the drinks flowed. Alison hadn't been part of the 'in crowd' in college and was surprised when one of its members came over to chat. Jason was his name. Typically the tall fair and handsome type, but he knew it. Alison was flattered to have been singled out and even more so when he offered to get her a drink. After that, it all went a bit hazy. She remembered leaving the pub with Jason, but not how she got home.

Work had started almost as soon as she had finished college and long before her results came out. She loved it. Being treated like an adult, having a wage; this was life. Her mum had become easier to live with since she could produce rent and board. Her work was going to release her one day a week for the course. She would have to use her own time for the additional study but they would pay both the tuition and exam fees. It was hard; doing a day's work and then studying in the evening, but it was a routine she was familiar with from college.

Then one week she had a touch of food poisoning. She struggled into work and as long as she nibbled on a ginger biscuit kept the nausea at bay. When the sickness extended into the second week, she made a doctor's appointment. She'd obviously picked up a bug from somewhere.

The doctor listened to the symptoms and then asked, "Do your breasts feel more sensitive than usual, or have you put on a bit of weight?"

Alison was perplexed. She had put on a bit of weight; her office skirt had got a little tighter, but she thought it was because of the ginger biscuits.

"I think you might be pregnant."

The air left her lungs and her head swam. She was going to faint. She was going to be sick. The doctor swiftly pushed her head between her knees and gently stroked her hair. After a few minutes, she felt she could sit up. "I can't be. I've never…" She trailed off.

"All right. Let's do a pregnancy test to get rid of that idea then." She gave Alison a typical chemist pregnancy kit. "All you need to do is wee on the end of the stick. It will take about a minute to tell you. Go and use the bathroom and come back with the result."

Alison's legs felt like they wouldn't take her anywhere, but she staggered to the toilet. She read the instructions and did what they said. She wasn't pregnant. Not even her mum believed in the Immaculate Conception and she was a rigid Catholic. The minute took forever and she looked. These days you don't have to worry about blue lines, two lines, it just says 'pregnant'. And it did. She gazed in disbelief. She couldn't be. She hadn't been with a boy. She hadn't had many boyfriends and those she had dated they'd never gone beyond a bit of heavy petting.

Then her mind swam back to the college leaving party. In fact, to the day after. She had felt a little sore between her legs, a bit of an ache in her lower stomach. She'd thought it must be that time of the month and thought no more about it. That thought was the moment she realised she hadn't had a period since the party. 'Oh, God. Had Jason…? How come she didn't remember? With slow, dragging steps, she returned to the doctor's office. She knew from the look on Alison's face what the result was. "You said you have never…had sex?"

Alison nodded. "I got drunk at a party. I must have… I don't remember," she wailed.

"Do you know who the father is?"

"I could make a guess, but not for sure."

"Obviously, this is a shock. You need to have time to think about what you want to do. I have some leaflets here and the telephone number of a counsellor. You need to talk to your family, friends. Get as many viewpoints as you can. Please remember you are not alone in this. Come back and see me within a fortnight and we'll discuss the way forward."

What would she do? Although not a strict Catholic she had been brought up to believe that abortion was a sin. But she'd also been brought up to believe that sex outside of marriage was another one. How was she going to tell her mum and what would she say?

That last question was soon answered. "You dirty little slut. You get so drunk you don't even know who the father is. And don't tell me it was only the once. That's an old wives tale; getting caught the first time. Well, I don't want you and your shame in my house. I want you out by the end of the week."

It was Victorian. Draconian. But she was adamant. Alison went into work, unable to hide the puffy eyes and blotchy nose. One of the older women, Grace, took her to one side. "What's up, love?"

Alison was tempted to lie, but she needed help. Equally, she needed this job. "Will you promise not to tell anyone else?"

"As long as it's not criminal, I won't say a word to anyone else."

Alison told her the whole story. Even the party bit. Grace blew her cheeks out. "Are you going to go after this Jason?"

Alison shook her head. "I can't. I don't know for sure it was him, but it's the only thing I can think of. And who's going to believe a silly girl getting too drunk to know what she did?"

"Okay. You need somewhere to stay as the first move. Have you decided if you're keeping it?"

Alison nodded. "I can't have an abortion." She was grateful that Grace didn't try and talk her out of it. Or just talk around it.

"Right. I have a spare bedroom that you are welcome to stay in until the baby arrives, but when you're a mum you need to have your own space. And I'm too old for broken nights."

Alison looked at her in amazement. Grace continued. "I will only charge you for food, £20 sound all right?" Alison nodded again. "But the rest of your money you have to save up for a deposit on a flat. While you're with me we'll get your name down on the Council's housing list and some of the Housing Associations in Swanton. The next big thing you've got to do is to tell management."

Alison went white. She'd lose her job and the course. She'd lose everything.

Grace hugged her and said. "Do you want to continue with the training?"

Again Alison nodded. "So the plan is to continue with the course until the baby is born. Then take a year out for the baby and maternity and then re-join for the next year."

"Why would they accept that?" She asked. "I've not been with the firm that long. I haven't even finished my probationary six months. Won't they just dismiss me?"

"It's going to be tough, but if you go to them with the plan and you work like a Trojan between now and the baby's arrival, you might be pleasantly surprised. I'm not guaranteeing it. But you might."

And that's what she did. Never one to put unpleasant things off Alison made an appointment to see her line manager that afternoon. Her legs shook and trembled as she stood outside the office door. As a voice invited her in she took a deep breath and went in.

After some discussion with her line manager and a further discussion that he had with the senior managers, they were surprisingly supportive. Alison thought that maybe Grace had prepared the way, especially about the circumstances of her pregnancy. They agreed with the break in her course studies and to maternity leave on the understanding that she would stay on for an additional two years. She readily agreed.

The next step was to go and get her stuff from home. Grace offered to drive her and waited in the car whilst she went in. Her mum was home. Neither said a word to each other. Alison went into her room and packed as much as she could carry in her suitcase and rucksack. The last time she'd packed these was to go on a school visit to Spain, Madrid. How long ago that seemed now. Fortunately, in terms of her studies, the laptop was her own, paid for from a Saturday job when she was in year 10.

She looked around her. There were marks on the wall where the sticky tape had marked the wallpaper when she'd had pop posters lining the room. Her old children's books. Neatly arranged on the shelf, but not read in many years. They would have to stay. No room for any more memories. She took one last look and walked down the stairs. The suitcase knocking behind her. Her mother stood at the bottom of the stairs. Alison vaguely hoped there may be reconciliation, but that bubble burst as her mum said, "I'll have your door key."

Alison searched in her bag and found her fob. She peeled off the key to her home and silently handed it over. She left trailing her suitcase.

She lived with Grace and saved every penny. Enough to put a deposit on a flat being prepared by Old Swanton Housing Association. They'd taken over Harrington Hall. It had once been a factory and some big conglomerate had bought it with plans for swanky urban conversions. Unfortunately, the crash of

2008 put paid to that and the Housing Association stepped in and developed a more utilitarian set of flats.

By using social media sites, she managed to collect things for the baby's arrival. One woman, selling a cot, complete with sheets and quilt, also gave her some baby clothes when she found out Alison knew she was having a boy. Some of the 'free' sites were also worth investigating and Alison was able to put together enough stuff to equip a first-time nursery. Grace and the other women at work, once they found out about the baby, brought in baby clothes saying things like, "I saw this and thought your little one would look lovely." Or "I saw this and couldn't resist buying it."

By the time Robbie arrived, she was set up in number 1, Harrington Hall. Her 'proper' maternity present from work had been a buggy. Not brand new, but one with all the adaptions that meant she could use it in a hundred different ways. The few weeks before his birth Alison spent getting the nursery ready.

The first weeks were tough. Constantly fearful that she was doing something wrong. Not sleeping because the baby cried or dozing fitfully afraid she wouldn't hear him if he did cry. She even resorted to having a little mirror in the nursery so she could check, at least once a night, that he was still breathing!

Grace gave her motherly support, and she survived. Through her health visitor, she joined a Mother and baby group and found there the support and confidence to believe she was doing okay. It was so wonderful to hear other Mums talk about sleepless nights, or grizzling that you couldn't settle. Especially supportive were the first time Mums who didn't feel embarrassed voicing their own outrageous fears. Laughter was often the remedy and sharing was definitely the cure. Or that even mothers with several children to their names still found it nigh on impossible to get up, washed and dressed before mid-day. It did get easier. According to Grace, and some of the women in the group, Robbie was a good baby. Alison certainly found she loved the time she had with him but once he was old enough for childcare she went back to work. She picked up on her work and course very quickly and progressed well. It was never going to be easy; a baby and evening study, but she was determined that she would give her child the very best she could and that meant qualifications and a reputation for working hard and working well.

Chapter 4

"No, Robbie, you can't." Alison White looked and sounded as frazzled as she felt. It had been a hard day and now Robbie was having a whine. Her mousey brown hair had been tossed and turned by the wind and she looked dishevelled as well as tired. Her coat was many years old and those years of winter wear where beginning to tell.

"Oh, please Mum. Just one go?" Robbie was an energetic eight-year-old. He wore the grey trousers and green sweatshirt uniform of his school. The trousers were going to need a wash, and mend, as Alison spied another hole in the knees.

"Robbie, I've got your tea to sort out and then I have work to do. I don't have time."

Gabe poked his head around the edge of the lift door. "Mrs White? I could take Robbie up and down while you get his tea sorted if that's okay?"

"Oh, please, Mum."

With a sound of deep resignation, Ms Alison White agreed. "I'll call when his tea's ready."

"Thanks, Mum." Robbie scampered to the lift. Because he lived on the ground floor he never got to ride the lift like everyone else in the block. Even little Jenny Earniston got to ride and she wasn't even five yet.

Gabe walked in behind Robbie, in time to see him shuffle his bottom into the leather chair. "Right. Ready? Off we go." Gabe pressed the button for the third floor. Slowly and with much creaking the lift lurched into action, rising no faster than the tortoise in the story.

"How was school today?" Gabe asked.

Robbie wriggled in the chair and looked down at his feet so that Gabe had a perfect view of the parting in his gold-brown hair. "Okay." His voice had little enthusiasm in it.

"Just 'okay'? You don't sound too sure."

Robbie squirmed some more.

Gabe just looked. There was something in that look that opened the door on Robbie's day. He looked up and fixed his clear blue eyes on Gabe. "Miss, told me off today. She said I was talking too much."

"And were you, talking too much?"

"Well, I was talking, but I was asking Johnnie Buller what a word was and Miss caught me."

"Did you tell her why you were talking? Did you explain?"

"Nah. The others would've thought I was a thicko."

"I'm sure they wouldn't."

Robbie gave him a sceptical look. "They would. They all laugh coz I can't read as good as them lot." He scratched nervously at a scab on his finger.

The lift had reached the third floor and the doors opened. "Do you want to get out and look at the view?" Gabe asked. Robbie would spend forever looking out across Swanton's vista if allowed. He was fascinated to work out where places he knew were. He could even make out his school if he stood on tiptoes.

"Yeah. That'd be great."

They went and stood by the large corridor window. It wasn't a beautiful view, but it showed Robbie his home town in all her different aspects. The grandeur of the town hall, just visible on the skyline. Well, the central dome was visible. Then there was the shopping centre. They were almost in line with the High Street and could watch people hurrying home, dashing in and out of the shops. Robbie's own Mum had been one of them only a few minutes ago. At the far end was the shopping centre. It had been built in the late sixties or early seventies and was typical of the brutalist concrete style of that era. Now the once pristine white concrete was soiled with black and grey streaks of air and water pollutants. In places, the inner metal rods to strengthen each block was rusting and brown and orange smears merged with the others. The town council were torn at the moment between those wanting to pull it down and start again and those who wanted to preserve it as a representation of that architectural style.

At the other end of the corridor, a duplicate window showed the other side of Swanton. Here they could make out the last of the industrial buildings that had once made Swanton rich and famous. There was the canal. Now no more than an unloved waterway, but once upon a time, it had bustled with barges. On the far side of the Swanton Park were the buildings of the rich Victorian and Edwardian factory owners. Their double-fronted homes were now subdivided into student flats. Swanton College had been the saviour of many of the older buildings of the town: repurposing and redesigning for the twenty-first century.

As they were taking in the view Gabe asked, "Do you practice your reading, Robbie?"

"Nah. I'm supposed to read at home, to Mum, but she's always busy and she gets stressed out."

"So what does your teacher say?"

"Oh, I dunno." Robbie scuffed his feet, taking another layer of leather off his black school shoes, and avoided eye contact.

"Robbie, you know you can tell me. I won't tell your mum or your teacher."

Robbie took a huge breath. "Well, sometimes I say I forgot to take my book home. Or I say I left my book at home and sometimes I tell her we were out so I couldn't do it." His face was neither triumphant nor cast down. This was just the way of it.

Any further discussion was prevented by the echo of Mrs White's voice up the lift shaft. "Robbie, tea."

"Come on then, Robbo. Let's get you to your mum and tea."

On the way down, Gabe changed the subject and talked about Robbie and his football. Like many boys Robbie's age he was mad about it.

At the ground floor, the lift doors drew back and revealed Mrs White, foot tapping. She had changed out of her coat but still wore her office clothes. Black pencil skirt, blue and white-striped blouse and sensibly heeled black shoes. She looked every bit the office manager she was.

"Come on. Robbie. Your tea's on the table."

"Brill!" Robbie went to dash off.

"Hang on a minute. Don't you have something to say?"

"Oh, yeh. Sorry. Thanks, Gabe."

"No problem." Robbie barely heard him as he ran indoors. Nothing gets between a boy and his food.

Memoir of an Idiot

I was thinking about my own schooling today; listening to Robbie explain how he tricked his teacher. I was lucky, I wasn't one of the bad lads but no high flyer either. My best, or favourite teacher, was my tutor in secondary school, Mrs Axton. Perhaps I should have gone back to school and tried to have a word with her when things started going wrong after Mum went away and Gran wasn't really here anymore. I had so many chances back then. What an idiot I've been to squander them all.

I like Robbie, I think he's a good boy. His mum is Mrs White on the ground floor. She seems very nice but very self-contained. Always in a rush. Things to do. It must be hard work being a full-timer and looking after an energetic eight-year-old. Like all boys that age he's always on the go. He told me today that to protect his mum, although he didn't say it like that, he lies to his teacher about his reading book. Apparently, he's supposed to read it to his mum but he says she has her own work to do. I remember one of my favourite things to do with Gran was read to her. Sometimes we took it in turns, reading a page each, and then as I got older, a chapter each. That's what Robbie needs. I don't think he's a stupid or lazy boy but he does need some outside help. Looking at his situation makes me realise how lucky I was that I had Gran. Mum would have been like Mrs White, far too busy putting food on my plate and a roof over my head to hear me read. I had all that support and never really appreciated the fact before today.

Chapter 5

Gabe gave some thought to Robbie and his reading. He didn't know Robbie well but what little he did know made him believe that Robbie was an intelligent boy, but not developing his reading was going to pull him back if it wasn't already doing so. Was this an area he could help with? Is this what Michael meant? He shook himself vigorously and told himself, "Forget what Michael said. Could you help this boy?"

If Robbie had an adult to read to each evening would it help? It would certainly mean that he could stop lying to his mum and his teacher. It would also take pressure off his mum. And, hopefully, it would help Robbie with the rest of his schooling. He remembered Mrs Axton saying, one day when he was bemoaning having to do English, "If you can read and write well you'll always get on in this world."

The following morning Gabe tried to attract Mrs White's attention as she was heading off to work. Robbie had been collected by a friend and his mum a few minutes earlier.

Mrs White was on her way to the outer doors when Gabe called her back. "Eh, Mrs White. Could I ask a favour?"

She turned back. "Call me Alison. Mrs White sounds like my mum."

"Thanks, err, Alison. It's just that I am doing a course at the local college in Community work and one of my assignments is to hear a youngster read for six months. Would you mind if I asked Robbie to be my reader? If that's okay with you?"

Alison looked blank for a few seconds. "You want Robbie to read to you? Where? In my flat?"

"Errm, I was thinking more like in the lift. Then I can do my job and not interfere with whatever you need to do."

Alison blushed. "Look, I don't mean any offence, but I don't know you from Adam. A quick up and down in the lift is one thing, but, what, half an hour just you and him."

Gabe stepped back and put his hands up, palms outward. "No, it's okay. No offence taken. It was just an idea. I should have given it more thought. Sorry." With that, he stepped into the lift and pressed a random button.

Alison stood there for longer. Had she made a mistake? Gabe seemed like a nice man, but what did she really know about him? Robbie liked him. But you hear so many stories these days. Nice men molesting small children. She shook herself. No not a good idea.

In the lift, Gabe was mortified. Not because Mrs White, Alison, had questioned his respectability. He really did understand where she was coming from and admired her defence of Robbie. No, he was angry at himself for not thinking all the ramifications through.

Chapter 6
Miss Ilene James' Story

Miss Ilene James looked around her new flat. It was pleasant enough. Plenty of light from the south-facing window. Only the one-bedroom, but why would she need two? She had no family and most of her friends were either dead or with serious mobility issues. No, a one-bedroom flat was fine. Large enough to move around in, small enough to keep clean with little effort. She would be doing her own cleaning and shopping, thank you very much. Even now she bristled at the thought of the young woman who had tried to foist a home help on her. "Send her to someone who needs it. I don't." She had been quite adamant. She looked out of the window. She could see down to the canal. It was a discarded place now, but she had known it when the barges still used it. Her first job was in Etherington's Ceramics. She had loved the place and was sad to leave. Sad to leave the job. Sad to leave Mr Etherington. But it was so many years ago, nearly sixty. So much has changed.

She'd had her fair share of lovers and the gaiety of life, but no one she wanted to stop with. Her work, as a personal secretary to a myriad of successful businessmen; and yes, they were all men, had given her travel in this country and around the world. She'd had amazing experiences; seen breath-taking sights; met with fascinating people. She had had a good, no, a great life. And this little setback was not going to put a dampener on it.

She'd not been profligate. Money was saved and invested. Unfortunately, her choice of investments let her down and she had been badly hit by the 2008 crash. At the age of seventy-eight, she found she was forced to sell her home and look for somewhere smaller to buy. The Old Swanton Housing Association offered a part rent, part mortgage contract that she invested the last of her house money in. If she ever needed a Care Home the state was going to have to fund it. But she'd fight tooth and nail before she let that happen.

Miss James looked around her new flat once again. At least she'd been able to bring her beloved Swanton ceramics with her and her books. She didn't possess a great deal. Even less since she'd had to downsize to move to this flat. A three bedroom semi for a one-bedroom flat. Quite a diminishment. She gazed at her ceramics and then at her books. They were old friends. Some read many times. You can never be lonely with a good book, she assured herself.

Chapter 7

There was little breeze that morning, and the sun had deigned to show its face. Gabe thought Miss James might well decide to take a walk, so after the workers had gone he left the lift on the third floor. Yes, he was right in his guess. Miss James' front door swung open wide and she slowly appeared pushing a three-wheeled walking frame. With careful steps, she pushed it before her and once clear of the door frame turned and pulled the door closed.

She wore a fetching blue beret, which made her snow-white hair even more striking. Her black wool coat was done up to the top with a blue silk scarf peeking above the collar. A red poppy brooch was her only adornment.

At that moment she reminded Gabe of his own Gran. Even to go to the local shop she would be properly attired. "If your hair is combed, your shoes polished and a hanky in your pocket you're fit to see anyone." That had been her mantra. He smiled at the memory and felt that familiar ache in his chest as he remembered that she was no longer with him.

"Good morning Miss James," Gabe hailed from the lift.

She waved a black-gloved hand and adjusted the long strap of her handbag which went over her shoulder and across her chest. Slowly, but deliberately, she made her way towards the lift. Gabe waited patiently. Once inside she turned with her back to the leather chair and carefully lowered herself down. Once Gabe was sure she was settled he started the lift.

"Going anywhere nice today, Miss James?" he asked.

"I am going to see old friends. The weather today makes a short walk and long conversations ideal."

Gabe knew that this meant Miss James was going to visit the cemetery. It was less than fifty metres from Harrington Hall and involved no crossing roads and negotiating curbs.

"Have you anyone, in particular, you plan to visit today?"

"Tomorrow is my old boss's birthday, but I don't expect I'll get out tomorrow, so I will go and see him." She settled herself back into the embrace of the chair. "Perhaps also Mrs Grimshaw. We worked together about forty-five years ago and we kept in touch. Mind you, she is a one for the gossip."

It never failed to amuse Gabe that Miss James spoke about the dead in the present tense. To her, they were as alive as he was. He knew she would wander from grave to grave, and she would have a conversation with the deceased. To those around her, it may have sounded one-sided, but for her, their replies were as clear as a bell.

Once the lift doors opened Gabe preceded Miss James to the outside doors and when she was ready he opened them wide so she did not have to negotiate them on her own. With a cheery backward wave, she set off.

Memoir of an Idiot

Miss James went for a walk to the cemetery today. She does remind me of Gran in her heyday before it all went wrong. I suppose things started to change just after my eighteenth birthday. Mum had completed her OU degree and had got a job with a firm in Manchester. Now, this was great news except it meant I had to decide whether to go with her, and leave my apprenticeship, or stay. If I stayed I wouldn't be allowed to keep the flat, the council said it was a family flat and I needed to leave. The obvious answer would have been to stay with Gran but she'd been going downhill fast in the last couple of years. I hadn't really noticed it at first; sometimes she'd ask me two or three times what I wanted for tea or she'd forget to put sugar in my coffee. I just thought it was old age, old people get forgetful. It was Mum who pointed out that Gran wasn't that old and that something serious was going on.

Mum eventually persuaded her to go and see her GP and then a memory Clinic bod. In short, she had Alzheimer's and it was progressing quite fast. In less than a year, she couldn't go out on her own and she'd become incontinent. There were yellow stickers on all her cupboards and drawers: food cans in here; underwear, etc. Then she started going out and getting lost. Four or five times the police brought her home. Mum said Gran needed to be looked after and got Social Services involved.

Mum was quite brutal with them. She told them she was moving away with her career and that she wasn't having her eighteen-year-old son having to deal with his Gran's incontinence. I think at the time I felt angry with everyone, but especially Mum. I thought she was heartless, putting Gran after herself, but I also felt guilty because I didn't want to be the one to look after Gran either. In the end, Gran was given a place in a home not far from the town centre. I visited her a lot to start with. The place seemed okay and the staff were nice enough but after quite a short time it wasn't Gran anymore. Sometimes when I went in she looked frightened of me. Other times she would ignore me. The staff said not to worry, it was all part of the disease but it felt personal. How could she not remember me when we'd spent so much time together? How could she let her onetime beautifully cut hair and made-up face disintegrate to this old woman? It wasn't fair. It feels childish now to say, it wasn't fair, but if I'm going to reflect on my past I need to accept what I remember and what I remember from this part of my life is how self-centred I was.

Chapter 8

Ginny Cole's Story

Ginny Cole sat at a table swamped in paperwork and stared sightlessly out into the darkening garden. But she wasn't there. She was thirty years away; standing on the deck of their honeymoon cruise ship. So much joy and laughter. They were full of optimism, full of love, full of life. But not anymore.

She came back to the room and lifted a cut-glass tumbler of liquid gold to her lips. She didn't really like the taste of whiskey, but at least feeling the warmth that trailed down inside her, made her realise that she was alive. For everything else, she felt numb. Nothing mattered. No one mattered.

She hadn't had time to prepare. One minute Graham was here and then not. A massive stroke, they said. Probably dead before he hit the floor. So he'd gone and left her. A vibe of anger twisted in her stomach. And he'd left her with all these debts. He had always taken care of the finances. Told her not to worry. He had it under control. Well, it looked like his debts were a raging fire. He'd kept dousing them with small amounts of cash, but never enough to clear them and now they all needed paying.

She sat forward again and looked at the final piece of paper she had been working on. She would have to sell the house. It wasn't quite mortgage-free, but at least he had kept up the payments on their home. Not so his business premises, his tool hire, or life insurance. Dave, his only employee wanted to take over the name and work, but couldn't afford to unless the debts were paid. The business was going to need most of the capital from the house. So where would she live?

What about her job? She'd been gearing up for retirement. She loved teaching but the pace was a young person's game these days. And, if she was totally honest, this final assault on her resilience had laid her bare. She'd seen too many teachers keep on at the chalk face because they had to. They hated the job and many, by the end, hated the kids too. No, she couldn't do that.

She would need to move into Swanton. Town lets were cheaper and more frequent. Perhaps a flat in one of those mid-rise blocks on the edge of the canal. Perhaps if Dave could pay a monthly amount for buying Graham's business, and with whatever she could release from her teacher's pension, she could cope. Not rich, but at least comfortable.

She downed the rest of the whiskey and pulled a face. Whatever she was going to do would have to wait until tomorrow. Talk to the bank. Talk to Dave. Talk to Graham's creditors. Talk to school. So many people to negotiate with. She put her forehead on the table. So much to do.

Chapter 9

No sooner had Gabe returned to the lift, he was called to the second floor. It could only be Mrs Cole. Mrs Davies had gone out in time to drop Jenny off for school, before going on to her job in the local chemist.

It was Mrs Cole. Gabe referred to her as Mrs but wasn't sure if that was so, but she had never corrected him. There she waited in her usual plum coloured waterproof and sensible shoes, she wasn't taken in by the sun's appearance after days of rain. Gabe would guess that she was of mixed heritage. Her skin tone was exactly the same colour as the latte he so loved if he treated himself to a shop coffee. Her eyes were very dark. So much so that he couldn't make out the iris from the pupil.

Mrs Cole gave a bright smile as Gabe's face appeared. "Morning Gabe. Have you been busy this morning?"

"Not really. Miss James has just gone out and I helped her with the outside doors."

Mrs Cole smiled and her eyes sparkled. "Is she off to talk with her friends at the cemetery?"

"I think so," Gabe tried not to talk in detail about any of his lift guests. Somehow he felt that his lift was a bit like the confessional; whatever was said stayed within its ancient walls.

Mrs Cole nodded and the sides of her stylish bob swung gently. Her deep brown hair had lines of silver in it that reminded Gabe of the veins in marble. There and part of the design, but not intrusive.

"Well, I, for my sins, am off to the dentist."

Gabe pulled a face of sympathy. Like most people, the dentist was something to be endured as infrequently as possible.

"No, it's fine. Just a check-up." She laughed. "I know I sound strange, but I don't mind going to the dentist. My husband, on the other hand, would insist that I go with him; even for a check-up. In any other respect, he was such a man's man. But the dentist had him back to childhood," she continued to smile, but a little more wistfully.

Gabe saw her give herself a mental shrug and she was back in the lift. "After that, I'm going to lunch with some of my old colleagues from work. I pity the restaurant staff: five older women, all teachers, all talking the hind leg off a donkey and all with that 'don't give a damn' attitude that comes with age! We will talk a lot; drink a lot and laugh a lot."

The lift had landed and as she stepped out Gabe smiled and said, "I know you're going to have a wonderful day. Enjoy it. You deserve it."

She smiled an acknowledgement and turned when she came to the outer doors and waved. Gabe waved in return. The more he saw of Mrs Cole the more he liked her. Now was going to be some downtime. Unless Captain Clive on the third floor decided to take a jaunt out, Miss James would probably prove to be his next passenger, as Gabe knew that Sam Freedman was on his twelve hours shift at the local hospital. Gabe had some admiration for Sam. He was apparently, guessing from his non-Swanton accent, far from home, living alone and making a success of it. It made Gabe feel even more ashamed of his own past actions. He'd allowed the loss of his Gran and his Mum moving away to completely derail him. Gabe's guilt knew no bounds. He knew he had a lot to make amends for.

With that in mind, he decided he needed to give some thought to the Robbie and reading situation. Robbie obviously needed to practice his reading more. He, Gabe, felt that supporting Robbie was an important role. Mrs White, Alison, equally obviously didn't have the time. He understood. She was a single working parent. There were never enough hours in the day for them.

He remembered how fraught his mum would get after his dad died. What was that Janice Joplin song his dad used to play, the chorus went something like, "You don't know what you've got 'til it's gone," well that was certainly true. He'd thought time with his Gran would always be there.

But what to do about Robbie? He had told a white lie about the course and the community work. Although when he thought about it, Michael had given him Community work to do. He wanted to help Robbie and he wanted to help Alison. As far as he could see there were few options: he could go into their flat if she didn't mind, but he couldn't keep an eye on the lift or he needed a chaperone.

Chapter 10

As anticipated Miss James was the next visitor to his lift. The fresh air had put some colour in her cheeks and she looked like she had enjoyed her meetings. Her pace was almost jaunty as she appeared at the top of the path to the doors. Gabe ensured he was there first to handle them so she could manoeuvre her walker in first.

"Thank you, Gabe. They're not designed for these silly walker things." Miss James waggled her frame as she got herself through the doors.

Gabe smiled. "Did you enjoy your walk, Miss James?"

"Oh, very much so. Talked to a few old friends and met a very nice young man tidying the beds. I do enjoy talking to my dear ones but a fresh face and some real conversation do make a difference."

Once again Gabe was struck by the grip Miss James really did have on reality. So often she sounded like she was away with the fairies and then she would say something that made you realise she was with you all the time. Especially when it was accompanied by a grin, as this comment was.

"Do you ever get talking to the other residents?" Gabe asked.

"No, not really. Perhaps a 'hello' if I see them out, but no. I'm not good with people. I'm better with children. Always wanted children, but it wasn't to be." There was no self-pity in her voice. Just a statement of fact.

Gabe's head suddenly fizzed with a brilliant idea. Well, that's how it seemed to him. He waited until Miss James had got herself comfortable in the armchair and the lift was on its journey and then he broached the subject of Robbie and reading. Once again he indulged in a half-truth and told her the situation with Robbie and Gabe 'needing' to hear him read and Mrs White understandably being worried.

"So, I was wondering, Miss James, could you be a chaperone? For when I hear Robbie read. You could sit in your chair, with a book if you want to, and I would work with Robbie."

Miss James looked him in the eyes. She kept her gaze steady. Her pale grey eyes didn't blink. Gabe thought she was looking through to his soul. Then she spoke. "May I have some time to think about that? How often would you need me to sit?"

Gabe hadn't considered time commitment. He realised that, again, he had gone off without thinking through all the ramifications. "I would imagine if I heard him read every weekday evening, do you think that would be enough? Too much?"

Miss James nodded. "Um. Keep it to school day evenings. That would be sensible."

The lift had arrived on the third floor. As she left Miss James said, "Come to my flat at nine tomorrow morning after all the workers have gone. You will have my answer then."

Gabe watched her slow and careful journey back to her door and the reverse proceedings for entering. Was he asking too much of her? He didn't know how old she was but she was older than his Gran had been when she died. He salved his conscience with the thought that if she did say yes she would be gaining some company of an evening. Would she like that? He was making a lot of assumptions here. Miss James gave a last look back and nodded as she stepped through her door. Gabe waited for it to close.

Memoir of an Idiot

I think I might have found a solution to the Robbie problem. I quite understand Mrs White's concerns. You read so much in the papers about young children being molested. Doesn't mean I didn't feel a bit embarrassed, and if I'm honest, a little angry, that she'd think that of me. But she doesn't know me. Let it go.

Anyway back to my plan. I have asked Miss James if she'd like to chaperone us, in the lift. She says she'll think about it and I've got to go and see her in the morning. But I think she'll say yes. She's like my Gran, up for a challenge! I hope she does say yes. I know it will be good for Robbie if we can persuade him to come and I also think Miss James will get something out of it. She must get lonely in her flat. Although Gran said she never felt lonely, she always had plenty to do. One of her sayings was 'Idle hands make the Devil's work'. How true that turned out to be.

Chapter 11

Gabe was concerned that he was going to be late to Miss James' as, unusually, Mrs Davies and Jenny were late going to school. Apparently, it was some sort of festival and Jenny was part of an assembly being held for the parents.

"It's being held in the primary school," Mrs Davies explained. "It helps to get the rising fives," she nodded towards Jenny sat in the leather chair with her legs outstretched, "used to going into their new school."

"And I am going to give presents to the poor people," Jenny chimed in.

"It's a tin of carrots and some rice pudding!" Mrs Davies added, "The school is collecting for one of the food banks in Swanton." She shook her head. "Who would have thought, in this day and age, we would be needing to support food banks!"

Jenny explained to Gabe. "It's a bank where you put in food and other people can take it out. Not like a proper bank where you put your money in but no one else can have it." She looked to her mother for assurance that her explanation was right. Mrs Davies smiled and nodded.

"Well done you," Gabe said, "have you got to say anything in your assembly?"

Jenny nodded and shuffled off the chair. She stood up straight. "I have to say: I am an ear of wheat. You can make flour for your bread from me. And I have to hold up a picture of an ear of wheat." She mimed her actions whilst she talked.

"That was brilliant," said Gabe.

"She's been practising every day for the last week," smiled her mother.

The doors opened and Jenny skipped out, followed by Mrs Davies. Words were exchanged at the outer doors and Jenny called back, "Thank you, Gabe."

"My pleasure. You'll be a star," Gabe called after her.

It was just nine when Gabe pushed the doorbell to Miss James' flat. He waited and eventually heard the creak of the walking frame. The door opened.

Miss James turned around and went back inside calling over her shoulder. "Come in. Shut the door."

Gabe did as instructed and followed Miss James into her main room. He was struck by the amount of light spilling through the window. He had forgotten that these flats faced south and Miss James flat was aglow with light. Under the window was a small armchair, obviously, Miss James spent time watching the world from her eerie. One wall was shelved out and was lined with books. From where he was Gabe couldn't see the titles, but they looked like well-read books. Not books just for the purpose of display.

Miss James had sat down in a large armchair at an angle from both the fire and the television screen. Another, less worn chair, sat opposite. She indicated for Gabe to take that seat. From this new perspective, he could see that behind Miss James was a beautiful display cabinet full of china tea and dinner services. Gabe didn't know a lot about such things, but he thought it looked like some of the Swanton chinaware, famous in the early nineteen hundreds. He had seen a leaflet about it in the Tourist Information place when he was trying to get a handle on his new home.

"Well, Gabe, I have given your proposal a good deal of thought, and on the surface, I can't see any great problems."

Gabe was about to say 'Thank you', but Miss James held her hand up.

"However, I would like to discuss the matter with Robbie's mum, before agreeing to your idea."

"Okay. Shall I ask her to come and see you?"

"Yes, please. I know she is a busy young woman so would you ask her to pop up when it is convenient this evening. It will only take ten minutes."

"You will explain that it is something to help me, won't you? I don't want Mrs White to think that I am criticising her and the way she is bringing up Robbie."

"No. I shall be tact itself. I know many people think I'm a dotty old woman." Gabe made to interrupt, but she batted his denial away. "I know they do, and I help them in that opinion. But I can be quick-witted enough when I want to be!"

Gabe grinned, "I've often thought that, myself."

Miss James returned the grin, "Right, you speak with Mrs White then."

"Will do, Miss James and thank you for considering the matter."

Chapter 12

Gabe was on the lookout for Robbie and his mum that evening and as soon as he saw them appear at the outer doors he went and positioned himself outside the lift.

Robbie was the first one to see him as his mum negotiated the doors with her shopping and briefcase. "Hello, Gabe. Can I have a ride?"

Alison looked a little uncomfortable as she realised Gabe was waiting to speak to her. To give her time to settle Gabe addressed Robbie's question, "That's up to your mum."

"Err, yes. Thank you, Gabe." With a whoop of delight, Robbie ran to the lift. Alison went to turn away to her own flat when Gabe called. "Mrs White, err, Alison. Could I have a word, please?"

Alison turned back. She was not happy to be in this position again and her face spoke volumes. She settled her shopping bags on the floor but retained hold of her briefcase.

"Please, believe me when I say I understand your concerns about Robbie being alone with me for any length of time. I really do. So I wondered if you would consider letting me do it if I had a chaperone."

Alison laughed. It sounded like something out of Jane Austen. "You mean some little old lady sat in the corner of the lift watching you and Robbie?"

Gabe smiled. "Err, yes, actually. Miss James, on the third floor, has said she may be the chaperone, but she would like to talk to you first."

"Is that the old lady with the walking frame? She's a bit…" Alison trailed off not sure of the correct adjective.

"She's not as batty as she lets on. Honest! Would you speak with her? She says any time that's convenient this evening. It'll only take ten minutes."

Alison paused and pursed her lips as she was thinking.

"Okay. I'm going to put this shopping indoors and then go and see Miss James. You and Robbie are happy to admire the view from the third floor while I'm in with her?"

Gabe nodded.

Alison turned and rummaged in her briefcase for her key. While she opened the door Gabe picked up two of the shopping bags and handed them to her. As she disappeared down the corridor of her flat he placed the third one inside the door.

Robbie's voice called out. "Come on, Gabe. Where are you?"

"On my way. Just helping your mum with her shopping. She's going to have a ride as well and go and see Miss James."

As Gabe entered the lift Robbie whispered, "The boys at school say she is a loony. She talks to dead people. They're frightened of her."

"No, she's just talking to herself. Don't you do that sometimes? I know I do. So are you afraid of her, Miss James?"

Robbie seemed to give this question serious consideration. "Nah. I think she's just lonely."

"I think you're right," Gabe agreed, surprised by his insight.

Alison entered the lift and Gabe pressed the third-floor button.

"Are you going to offer your mum the seat, Robbie?" Gabe asked.

"Err, Yeh, alright. Here you are, Mum," he jumped out and stood to one side.

"Thanks, Robbie. I must admit my feet are killing me," Alison said as she lowered herself down. Although Robbie had told her about the room Gabe had created in the lift this was the first time she had actually seen it. She rather liked the cosiness of it. She just felt a little uncomfortable with Gabe there. She knew he said he understood her misgivings, but it was still a bit awkward.

Robbie went and perched in the Captain's chair, his legs swinging backwards and forwards as the lift cranked its way to the top.

On the third floor, Alison knocked at Miss James' door and was admitted. Gabe and Robbie went to admire the view. The bright day was turning into a gloomy night and they watched the street lights begin to come on. The neon signs of the high street were garish against the grey dusk. People were black shadows suddenly attacked by flares of colour. The lights of the Town Hall lit up the dome and the top of the colonnades. It looked like something out of Disney. There must also be a match on at the local grounds because the floodlights were lit as well, throwing that side of town into an eerie blue glow.

Miss James' ten minutes was twenty, and so they transferred to the other window. Here the foreground was quite dark and little moved, but in the distance, the student flats were lit up in the old Victorian grand houses. Gabe wondered if

51

they had looked this illuminated in their heyday. Finally, Alison reappeared, shouting her thanks as she pulled the door closed behind her. Back in the lift, it was Alison who raised the topic of reading with Robbie. "Gabe needs to hear a young man read to him as part of his course. Do you think you could do that for him, Robbie?"

Robbie looked suspiciously at Gabe, who nodded and smiled. "It would really help me out if you would, Robbie. It's sort of like I have homework to do for my course at the college."

"And Miss James," Alison continued, "is also going to be here so she can listen as well. What do you think?"

The lift had reached the ground floor. Robbie wanted to make sure he'd got this right. "So, I'm going to read to Gabe and Miss James as well?"

"Well sort of. Miss James says she gets lonely reading by herself so she wants to set up 'The Lift Book Club'. You and she are going to be the first members."

Robbie noticed that Gabe looked as surprised as he did. "The Lift Book Club?"

Gabe recovered first. "What a fantastic idea. Come on, Robbie. This sounds like it could be fun."

Robbie wasn't so sure. "So it will be extra homework? For school?"

"Yes, but you already have reading homework, don't you?" Gabe asked. "So you will just be doing your homework in a different place."

"And I know you often want me to hear you read, don't you? This way there will be somebody available any time you like," added Alison.

Robbie still wasn't convinced. "But why in the lift? Why not in our flat or Miss James'?"

"The problem is that I can't leave the lift, so it needs to be here. And if we're going to call it The Lift Book Club, it needs to be here. Do you see?"

Robbie grudgingly agreed. "Yeh. Ok. But why not Jenny on the second floor? I'm sure she needs help with her reading." He was still looking for the loopholes.

Gabe gave the impression of seriously considering Robbie's proposal, and then sadly shook his head. "No, that's not going to work. She's too young. I need someone who can already read quite well." Gabe hoped the last sentence would appeal to Robbie's ego.

With a huge sigh, as though realising he was caught on all sides Robbie, said, "When do we start?"

Alison answered. "You start tomorrow right after you've had your tea, about 4:30. So don't forget to bring your book from school."

"That sounds like a great plan. What do you think?" Gabe asked again.

Robbie considered and said. "Okay."

Gabe still wasn't sure that Robbie was on board. They'd have to wait and see what tomorrow brought.

Memoir of an Idiot

Miss James has said yes to chaperoning the reading sessions. She's a clever old girl she's suggested that we create The Lift Book Club, I suppose so it doesn't sound quite like homework for Robbie and also explains why she will be there. I hope this works.

Back to my catalogue of stupidity. Mum was really good she helped me find a place before she left for Manchester. It was a room in a house, but one where the landlady lived as well, Mrs Gillespie. She had the two rooms downstairs, we all shared the dining room because she provided evening meals and breakfast and there was me and one other lodger in the rooms upstairs. It was quite nice. Both rooms were en-suite and there was Wi-Fi, so pretty good really. Mum said she would pay the rent and I would need to pay for the meals. That seemed really generous of her and meant I still had cash to go out with mates.

Mrs Gillespie was all right, but it was definitely a business relationship. She wasn't one for cosy chats once we'd eaten. Instead there would be an unspoken impatience for us to be gone so she could wash up and settle down for the evening. The other lodger was Barry Thomas. He must have been in his fifties, had been with Mrs G for more than ten years. He wasn't a great conversationalist either unless you were into trains. I know you shouldn't stereotype people but he really was exactly what I imagined a train-spotter to be like, thinning hair, stooped shoulders, glasses and the ubiquitous anorak.

The first few months were okay. Mum phoned most evenings and I had college work to do. It was the weekends that dragged. A lot of my mates had steady girlfriends and so they were usually playing football Saturday morning and then seeing the girlfriend in the evening. Sometimes, I'd meet up with them for a pint in the after-match celebrations or commiserations, but then they would have to leave. Sundays were a drag. It seemed like everyone had family stuff to do. For a while, I visited Gran, but that just got harder and harder. Then in college, I met a guy, Terry. I met him in the canteen and just got chatting. I can't even remember what we said. Then it seemed that Terry was always there. It took me quite a while to realise why he was there. I thought he was a late entry to a course, but he wasn't a student at all. He was a bit cagey about why he was there, once I'd sussed he wasn't doing a course but eventually he coughed to the fact that he came to college to sell gear, drugs. I'm not particularly naive about drugs. There had been kids at school that I knew where taking stuff, and not all of it low deal stuff like weed but it wasn't something I'd ever got involved in. Not that Terry tried to sell me any stuff, at first.

Chapter 13

The inaugural meeting of The Lift Book Club started promptly at 4:30pm on the following day. Gabe waited in the lift for the arrival of Miss James. When she had positioned herself comfortably in the armchair she took from her basket on the walker a little knitted blanket, which she tucked around her knees and a book. She had also taken the precaution of wearing a thick sweater and trousers. "I do feel the cold so," she said by way of explanation.

Once back on the ground floor Gabe arranged the half-moon table next to the wooden chair so that Robbie could stand next to him and rest his book on the table.

Robbie entered the lift with his school satchel. Not quite 'creeping like snail/unwillingly to school'. But not far off. He laid the satchel on the table and pulled out his book bag; within which was a reading book and a 'comment' book. He hadn't yet made eye contact with them nor acknowledged their presence. Gabe picked up the notebook. "What's this for, Robbie?"

"You have to write how many pages I have read and whether I am doing okay," deep suffering flavoured his words. He was determined not to enjoy this experience.

Gabe flicked through the last few written pages. He noticed that most of the entries were by Robbie's teacher. Sometimes she had written out words that Robbie had obviously struggled with. "Okay. I think I get this. So what're you reading at the moment?"

Robbie held up the book. "It's a baby book." His disgust was clear to hear.

"Okay. Well, let's see how quickly we can get you onto something you want."

With a deep sigh, Robbie opened the book. He placed his index finger on the page, beneath the first word. As he read so his finger moved. "Molly wanted Mum to play, not look for food for their supper."

Over his shoulder, Gabe could see the bright picture of a stylised rabbit and forest view.

Robbie turned the page, "Looking for food was boring. So she ss c a mm."

He was trying to sound out the word. Gabe waited a little longer. Robbie continued, "Scamp err ed. Scampered."

"Well done, Robbie. That's a tough word. Do you know what it means?"

Robbie shrugged his shoulders. "Well, what is Molly doing in the picture?"

Robbie looked. "She's running away." There was a tone of 'obviously' about his response.

"There you go then. Scampered means 'to run off'."

Robbie resumed and so the session continued. Miss James seemed deep in her book, but occasionally Gabe saw her peek over the top to check how Robbie was coping. In their half hour slot, Robbie had read the whole book. Having read the final page he snapped it closed.

"Right, so you had two words that you had a problem with. Let's see if we can find them and you have another go. Gabe found the offending words and Robbie read them cleanly."

Gabe addressed Miss James. "Well, Miss James. I don't know about you, but I think Robbie read that really well."

Miss James put down her book and looked at Robbie. "Yes, you did, Robbie. I am very impressed. I think you need to ask your teacher for a harder book. Not knowing only two words is very good and I think this book is too easy for you."

Robbie blushed and looked down. He tried really hard not to smile but Gabe could see the corner of his mouth lifting.

Gabe completed the notebook. "I've told your teacher that you've read the whole book and that you struggled with only two words, but could read them at the end."

Robbie took the notebook and his reading book and shoved them back into his book bag and then into his satchel.

Gabe opened the lift doors and Robbie left. Just as he stepped over the lip Gabe asked. "Are you okay with coming again tomorrow?"

Robbie turned and nodded his head. Not quite a smile on his face, but nowhere near the hangdog expression of earlier.

Chapter 14

It was with a little more enthusiasm that Robbie opened his book bag the following evening. He gave Gabe the notebook to read. There on the page, after Gabe's comment and the words, Robbie had struggled with, his teacher had affixed a gold star and written. *'Very good reading'*.

"Well done, Robbo!"

Robbie beamed. As he pulled out his new reading book he said, "I was allowed to choose this for myself."

"Okay. Before you start can I just check that you can still read the words you had problems with yesterday?"

Gabe flattened the notebook and pointed to each word. In turn, Robbie read them clearly.

"Right. Now for this new book."

The pointing finger appeared below the first word and Robbie began. Although his pace was steady Gabe noticed that he didn't stop at any punctuation marks or take any breaths. Instead, as he reached the end of the page he took in a deep breath and went to turn over the page. This hadn't been obvious with the previous book because there was only ever one sentence on each page.

Gabe stopped him. "Hang on a minute, Robbie. Can I just check something with you?"

Robbie stopped and waited, his shoulders slightly hunched.

"You read that first page without one mistake. Well done!"

Robbie's shoulders relaxed a little.

"I just want you to tell me about what you've just read. So what's happened so far?"

Robbie looked mystified. The question didn't seem to compute in his mind.

"Okay, so who is the story about?"

"Jack."

"Okay. And what has happened to Jack on the first page?"

Robbie still looked nonplussed. "Err." Robbie stopped and looked back down at the first page.

"See, Rob, there's no point in reading well if you're not taking in what's happening. And you might understand it more if you read with the punctuation. You know what punctuation is, don't you?"

Robbie nodded, "Full stops and that."

"Good so when you come to a full stop you should stop, take a breath, take a second to understand what you've just read. Yeh?"

Robbie shrugged again. His face a little sullen, "I guess."

"Come on then. Give that first page another go."

Robbie did give it another go and stopped as the punctuation indicated. When he got to the end of the page he nodded up at Gabe. "Yeh, I get it."

With being an older age group book, this one they did not finish in one evening. Gabe marked off the amount Robbie had read and that there were no words he had had difficulty with.

Just before he left Miss James said, "Thank you, Robbie. You read aloud really well. I got so interested in your book that I forgot to read mine. I look forward to hearing the rest tomorrow."

Robbie smiled. "Okay, Miss. See you tomorrow," and he turned and darted out through the doors.

As Gabe took Miss James back to her floor she remarked, "You can tell just from two evenings that he's a bright boy. He just needed that little bit extra. Well done, Gabe."

Gabe blushed. "Well, it's him doing me the favour, really."

Miss James smiled knowingly as she made her way out of the lift.

Memoir of an Idiot

The reading with Robbie seems to be going well, both in terms of Miss James being in the lift with us and Robbie's reading. I like Miss James' idea of calling it The Lift Book Club. It somehow makes it more acceptable. Robbie certainly doesn't seem to mind coming now. Really he was only reluctant on the first day, but now he can see it is making a difference he's all for it.

I thought a little later on we'd try alternate reading of pages like I used to do with my Gran. I used to like that because it made me feel I could read as well as she could. Hopefully, Robbie will feel the same.

Terry. Once I'd realised what Terry was up to I made it clear that I didn't do drugs. He held his hands up and reassured me he only dealt with those that came to him. And in fairness I never saw him approach anyone on campus, they always came to him. Anyway one day, I think I might have been moaning about how boring it was at weekends and he suggests that we meet up on Sunday. He and a few mates were into war-gaming. *The Full Monty*; maps and plans of real campaigns, small painted soldiers, the works.

To be honest, I wasn't sure. It sounded to me as weird as Barry the train-spotter, but I was lonely on Sundays, so I said yes. Terry's group had the use of one of the rooms in the local youth group building. There were five or six of them; the number varied, depending on who was available and which battle they were fighting. It really wasn't for me but it gave me a group to belong to. Everyone brought along a few beers and we sat and chatted when the battle was quiet.

It became a regular thing, war-gaming on a Sunday. Innocent enough and then Terry invited me to meet him and a few mates at his local, which wasn't that far from Mrs G's. So I did. And try as I might, looking back and wanting to be honest, I don't know how it developed from there. First, we were meeting on Sundays and the odd night in the week and then we were meeting most nights. First, it was just a couple of pints a night and then it was a skin full most nights.

I can't think about this now. It's making me feel sick.

Chapter 15

Mrs Cole was the first resident outside the originators of The Lift Book Club, to come across one of their sessions. She had been out with a friend to see a film and have afternoon tea. She looked surprised as she stepped in and saw Gabe and Robbie deep in a book and Miss James in the armchair.

"Hello. Is this a private party or can anyone join in?"

Robbie was quick off the mark. "It's our book club. The Lift Book Club. She can join can't she?" he appealed looking first at Miss James and then at Gabe.

"Well, I don't see why not," said Miss James.

"Are there any rules I need to know about?" asked Mrs Cole, surprised that her witticism had received such a response.

Robbie looked to the adults again. This time Gabe answered. "We haven't really made any rules, yet."

"We just come here and I read to Gabe," said Robbie.

"And it gives me company whilst I read," added Miss James.

"What a lovely idea!" exclaimed Mrs Cole, "Does your book club need any books? I have some children's history books and one," here she hesitated and reddened slightly, "I wrote myself about Old Swanton and the ceramic works."

Gabe wasn't sure if they wanted books. "Well, it's just reading books for Robbie, really."

"That's fine. These are for eight- or nine-year-olds, and the one I wrote when I was teaching year 6 because we did a project on Old Swanton."

"I for one, would be pleased to look at your book, my dear," said Miss James. "I worked in the last commercial ceramic factory in Old Swanton. Etherington's. I'd love to see what you've got."

And that decided it. The following day, true to her word, Mrs Cole arrived with half a dozen Goldberg's Children's History through the Ages books. They had been well used but their jackets were in one piece. Mrs Cole's own book was a tidily presented paperback with a picture of one of Old Swanton's ceramic factories on the front. For the time being Gabe placed them on the half-moon table, but he would need to find someplace else for them.

That evening Robbie came in promptly, but rather than getting his book bag out he took out a folded piece of A4 writing paper.

"What've you got there, Robbo?"

"Well. I was thinking about what Mrs Cole said, you know, about what our rules are. So I've made some rules. Look." And he handed the paper to Gabe.

Gabe read quickly. The paper was entitled:

The Lift Book Club
Rules

1. *You have to live in Harrington Hall*
2. *You have to come to read*
3. *You should be quiet in the lift when it is the book club*

"Well, that's a good start. What do you think Miss James?" Gabe handed the paper across to her. She took a moment to read it and then nodded.

"Good, but we need to add in something to Rule 1 because Gabe only works here, he doesn't live here."

Robbie pulled out a pen and put a line through Rule one and wrote underneath:

1. *You have to live or work in Harrington Hall.*

He showed the new rule to Miss James, who nodded her agreement.

"And we should have a book to mark down who comes each time. You know, sort of like a school register," suggested Robbie.

Gabe now nodded. "Okay. I think we can do that. The only thing I'm a bit worried about is where is everyone going to sit to read?"

"There are masses of room in here," said Robbie, throwing his arms wide. "We'll get some more chairs."

"I don't know about masses, but we could fit in another two smaller chairs, couldn't we Gabe?" Miss James asked.

"Well, yes, but I don't know where from. These," he indicated the present lift furnishings, "all came from skips."

"I think I might have the answer to that, but let's get on with Robbie's reading session. I want to know what's happened to Jack."

Later, when taking Miss James back to the third floor, she said. "If you could accompany me back to my flat, I think I may have just what we need for more seating in the lift."

Gabe followed her back to the front door and waited whilst she got herself in. "Come in Gabe. Leave the door. You'll need it open to take these bits and pieces out."

Miss James went into what Gabe guessed was a deep cupboard off the hall. Not only was it small but much of its content was boxes. Miss James had left her walker in the hall and was peering around and through the stacked items.

"Here they are. Gabe could you lift these two chairs out, please." She pointed to two wooden, collapsible chairs leant in one corner, "and there should be. Oh, there it is. And that footstool."

Miss James backed herself out the way so that Gabe could get the items mentioned. The chairs were well made and not too heavy. Gabe looked at them as he lifted them out.

"They're surprisingly comfortable, you know. I used to take them in the back of the car when a friend and I went out for a picnic. There's a table somewhere as well. But we don't need that."

The footstool was atop a tall cabinet and Gabe had to stretch up to reach it. It was a little four-legged, woven seated stool.

"What do you think, Gabe? Could they go in the lift without causing a clutter?"

"I think they're ideal. The chairs can go behind your armchair until we need them and the stool you can either put your feet up or Robbie might like to perch on it from time to time."

Chapter 16

The new arrangements for the lift were completed a few days later when Gabe brought in a small two shelved bookcase. It looked like it had once been a vanity or wall cabinet, but Gabe had removed the door and cleaned and painted the inside. Pat, the manager at the Hostel had allowed him to use up an old pot of paint so that he could spruce his skip find up. He placed the newly made bookcase to the back of the lift and its first occupants were the books donated by Mrs Cole.

Both Robbie and Miss James smiled their approval when they saw it. Robbie had asked his mum to type up the rule sheet in large letters and she had laminated it. Robbie asked if it could go up in the lift. Gabe stuck it to the wall above the bookcase.

"The only thing is Robbo," said Gabe. "Now we have the rules up other residents might want to join. Is that okay?"

"Yeh, course. But we need a register, don't we? We said last time, didn't we?"

"Okay. I'd forgotten that you mentioned a register before. If that's what you want. I'll bring in a book that we can use as our register. Right. No more timewasting. What are you reading today?"

Robbie's reading had gone from strength to strength. Even to the point where one Friday evening he came straight in from school to show Gabe a certificate he had received at school. It read, *'For the most improved reader this term'*. Gabe was delighted. "Fantastic, Robbo. What's your mum say?"

"She says I'm a brainbox and she's dead chuffed," Robbie said grandly.

"That you are, mate. Well done."

Later Miss James was shown the precious piece of card and was equally glowing with her praise. Robbie was torn between wanting to put the certificate up in the lift or having it in his bedroom. In the end, he opted for his bedroom. His reasoning being, "People might think I'm a show-off, mightn't they, Gabe?"

"Well, I see where you're coming from and it might make people think that they have to be good readers to join the book club, so, yeh. You put it in your bedroom."

Robbie's time in the lift often exceeded the thirty minute reading time. As she had said, Miss James was eager to read Mrs Cole's book about Swanton's ceramics and she had begun to draw Robbie's attention to different bits of information. It turned out that she had worked as the secretary for the owner of the last ceramics factory, a Mr Etherington. "Such a lovely man. Do you know he set up a voluntary savings scheme for his workers and they could draw it out whenever they wanted, but if they left it in all year they got their share of the interest?" Robbie began to use the footstool to sit alongside Miss James as she showed him pictures in the book. One evening she brought down a photo album. Many of the pictures were black and white, but they charted the life of Miss Ilene James.

"Cor! Is that you, Miss?" Robbie asked pointing to a stunning studio portrait with hand-painted tinting.

"Yes. That was me. I had that done for my twenty-first birthday."

Gabe looked and said, "You were certainly a looker in your time, Miss James. You must have been beating the boys off."

Miss James smiled brightly. "I certainly had my pick."

"But you're not married," Robbie chimed in.

Gabe glowered at him as though he should know better, but Miss James just laughed. "I didn't want to get married. I had my…"

Gabe thought she was going to say 'lovers' but she continued, "my boyfriends and had a lovely time. I think if I had been young today I would have lived with one. But that sort of thing just wasn't done in my day."

There were pictures of Miss James with Mr Etherington. He was a large man, with a King George V beard. Always dressed in a suit and tie. "He was a kind man with, what was once called, a sunny disposition," Miss James said.

*****

Mr Etherington and his secretary, Miss James, walked into the worker's canteen and instantly the noise level dropped. He wasn't in his usual three-piece suit. He had taken off his jacket and rolled his sleeves up, showing large hairy arms. His waistcoat hung wide and his tie was askew. Miss James looked miserable and kept glancing down at the open ledger she had in her hand.

All eyes turned their way and loaded forks were put back on the plates. They had been expecting to see him for a few days now. The rumour factory had been doing overtime, but they knew the business was struggling. You didn't need to be a qualified accountant to know that the orders weren't coming in as fast or as many as they had done in the past.

"Ladies and gentlemen, thank you for your attention." His baritone voice could be easily heard across the large echoing space. "I know you have all been worried about our business and I have come to you as soon as I had some news."

Everyone was on the edge of their seats. This wasn't going to be good news. Every fibre in Etherington's and Miss James' body told them so long before his words did.

"The bank has refused any further loans on the business and I have been unable to find a buyer who would keep the factory running. Etherington's will close at the end of this week."

No one stirred. This week! How were they going to cope? So many factories had already closed and unemployment was horrendous in Swanton. For some families, this was devastating news. They were all employed in Etherington's in some capacity; three or four wages would go in one week.

"All of you will get a settlement in lieu of notice. How much exactly I will be able to tell you by Wednesday; once Miss James and I have been through the final figures. In addition, many of you will have your savings scheme money and any interest on that."

There was a low murmuring that circled the room. Well, that would be handy. But how long would that last? Shoulders slumped. Some faces disappeared into hands. Some, men included, wept.

*****

"When he knew he couldn't get a bank loan to keep the factory going he called all the workers to a meeting and explained that Swanton ceramics was being closed down, but that if some of them wanted to buy some of the equipment and a kiln he would give them a building for nothing and the trade name. He was heartbroken and couldn't bear to think the name would die out."

Robbie's eyes were like saucers. "So everyone was going to be without a job?"

"Afraid so, Robbie. Over three hundred people, in fact. And that was just from the factory. When big employers go out of business lots of other firms suffer as well."

"I'm assuming some of the workers took him up on his offer? I've passed the little pottery place down by the river," Gabe interjected.

"Yes. Fifteen of them. Ten men and five women. The women were the best ones for the fine painting and detailed work. And they've survived. I know only in a small way. But Mr Etherington was so pleased that they took it on."

Other stories emerged as pages were turned and photographs were poured over. Gabe recognised that Robbie had an interest in the history of his home town and wondered if it extended further. It did. When Robbie announced that they were 'doing the Tudors' at school Gabe got him to read from the Tudor Age Goldberg's book.

Chapter 17
Kathy Davies' Story

They'd been friends forever. Thrown together by the common criteria of not fitting in. Kathy had found the backbiting and the self-absorption of most of the girls in her school wearying. Not that she was bullied. She was too uninteresting even for that. She sat at the front of the bus, on her own, every day, until the day John arrived. He was tall for his age and all hard angles. He didn't look like he wanted to sit next to her, but there was nowhere else. He dropped down hard into his seat, his sport's bag landing in her lap. She'd quite expected no apology or a grunt, but no, he was politeness itself and apologised profusely; making fun of his own clumsiness.

And it started from there. Small, inconsequential, chats led to longer and more thought-provoking talks. Although John would happily play football during a PE lesson he wasn't the type to want to spend every break time playing. He was just enough of a 'lad' to not be the focus of any bullying. A few made comments about the fact that he would just as happily go to the library and do his homework or chat to Kathy, but not enough to cause problems. He wasn't a threat to anyone and he wasn't a target. In time, people assumed they were an item and they did nothing to disabuse them of the idea.

At sixteen they both went on to college. Kathy to a Nursery Nurse qualification and John to continue with his interest in IT. By the time the next educational milestone came along, they had accepted themselves as a couple. Kathy went to work in a local nursery and John got an IT apprenticeship. Kathy sometimes, and only to herself, worried that there hadn't been the fireworks and heart-stopping moments that you saw on television or read in books, but, she told herself, this was a love born of friendship. And even though others were beginning to drop not so subtle hints about marriage and family, they both steadily ignored it all. They would do things in their own time.

By the time he was twenty-two John had successfully completed his apprenticeship and been invited by a start-up concern in Swanton to come on board as their IT consultant. At first, he went alone but missed Kathy; her common sense and her support. So it was practical measures, as much as love that saw them eventually get married. It was a small affair. Neither they nor their respective parents had money to burn, and after so many years of being together, there seemed little point in making a big song and dance about it. They started in a small two-room bedsit. They laughed because the second room was the bathroom! It was basic, but they coped.

In time the company took off and John was promoted. They couldn't afford an outright mortgage, but if Kathy carried on working, they could afford a part rent/part mortgage contract that some of the local housing associations were offering. That was their move to Harrington Hall. Although they hadn't discussed starting a family they had gone for a two-bedroom flat. However, when Kathy got pregnant John was not overjoyed. In part, it was finances, but as his father had said, "You rarely budget for a baby before it happens." They did manage and as soon as she could Kathy found work that she could fit in childminding around. Despite his initial misgivings Kathy was delighted to see that John adored Jenny. He had said that he had never seen himself as father material but this little bundle of joy occupied his heart in a way he could never have dreamt of. Bedtime stories and walks to the park. He loved every minute of it. They settled into stable family life. No dramas, just a steady, comfortable life together.

Chapter 18

As Gabe had predicted, the other residents, on seeing the book club's rules also became interested in becoming members. Jenny Davies became its first new member, according to Robbie's official register. When she understood that Miss James was also a constant member Mrs Davies lost no time in providing a few simple storybooks and Jenny each evening. So it became the habit that Robbie stood next to Gabe and read from his book on the table, whilst Jenny knelt on the footstool next to Miss James and read from the book Miss James had on her lap.

Jenny was an inquisitive child and often her own storytelling was interrupted by her distraction with Robbie's story. Suddenly he became aware that the second, piping voice had gone quiet and he'd become aware of Jenny's intense gaze as she listened to him read. For some reason, this embarrassed him and he would find himself stuttering through words he knew perfectly well.

Mrs Davies donated more books; these were from a local charity shop. "Five for a pound," she said. "You can't go wrong with prices like that, can you?"

Gabe's bookshelves were filling up.

One evening Robbie had finished his school book early and was browsing the books from Mrs Davies. "Gabe, is this the same Harry Potter as in the films?" Robbie held up two books from the Harry Potter series.

"Yes. Do you want to have a go at reading one? They might be a little hard for you. I think they're meant for older children."

"Which of these is the first one?" He waved the books about.

"I can't see the titles with you waving them about. But the first book is The Philosopher's Stone. Is that one of them?"

Robbie scrutinised the front covers and then put one back and clasped the other to his chest. "I'll be nine next birthday. It's my birthday in nineteen days. I'll try this one." He came and stood by Gabe and opened the book, flicking through the pages until he came to the one entitled 'Chapter 1'. Gabe quite expected Robbie to struggle with the names, if not some of the vocabulary, but in fact, he made a very good start.

"Well done, I thought you'd struggle with the Dursley name."

"Nah. I've heard the name in the films."

He did struggle with *shuddered* and *wrestled*, but sounded them out, once Gabe told him the *w* in *wrestled* was the same sound as the *w* in *write*. Jenny and Miss James had given up all pretence of doing their own reading and were listening intently to Robbie. The reading was interrupted by the arrival of Alison. "Sorry, everyone, but it's Robbie's Parents' Evening tonight and we need to head back to school. Don't we, Robbie?"

"Yeh," Robbie didn't sound enthusiastic.

"Come on then."

"Gabe, can I take this book home?"

"I don't see why not."

"But I've got to write it down. Like we do at school."

Gabe turned to the back of the register book and wrote up a page 'Loans' and added some columns. "Okay, Robbie you need to write your name in the first column, just Robbie will do. Then the name of the book in the next one and today's date in the third one."

Robbie did as asked. Alison waited not particularly patiently but seemed to understand that this was all very important to her son.

Having completed his loan registration Robbie turned to his mum. "I've just got to put this in my room."

Alison sighed, "Quickly then" and handed him the door key. To prevent Alison from feeling awkward waiting, Miss James said, "He really is enjoying his reading now, isn't he?"

Alison smiled, "He is. I even caught him reading in his room the night before last, even if it was after his light should have been out!"

Robbie returned a little breathless and handed the key back to his mum. "Come on then. It won't do to be late for your teacher, will it?"

*****

Alison and Robbie sat nervously waiting for his class teacher to be free to talk with them. Robbie squirmed, Parents' Evenings were no fun. They talked about you like you weren't there. Or if they did talk to you it was for you to agree that you weren't doing what you should be doing.

Alison was also squirming, on the inside. She always felt like the teachers were pointing out what a useless mum she was. And it just underlined her guilt that she didn't spend enough time helping him with his homework. Not because she didn't want to, but because she had her own 'homework' and that was what kept the money coming in.

Finally, Mrs Hart was free. They both sat down waiting for the onslaught. Mrs Hart looked at Alison and beamed. "I don't know how you've done it. Mrs White, but the change in Robbie in this last term has been amazing. His reading age has gone from under eight to eleven plus. Just in that short space of time!"

The rest of the evening passed in a blissful blur for both Robbie and his mum. He was working harder. Getting more right. Showing an interest. The praise kept coming. They left his school in a warm glow. "Well done, Robbie. That's the best Parents' Evening I have ever been to, and that includes my own time at school."

Chapter 19

The following day Gabe had two unexpected visitors to the lift. The British summer weather was living up to its reputation and Gabe had just put his wet jacket in the laundry room when he spotted Alison hovering outside the lift.

"Hi, anything wrong? Is Robbie okay?"

"Yeh, yeh. Robbie's fine. I just wanted to tell you about his parents' evening."

Gabe indicated that she should come in and take a seat. She sat in the leather armchair and looked around as though she hadn't really taken the lift's features in before. Her eyes lingered on Robbie's book club rules and smiled. "You know Robbie loves this book club."

"Well as a founding member, he is one of its stars."

"That's what his teacher said last night. Not about The Lift Book Club, but that Robbie was a star. She said that his reading improvement is remarkable and that it seems to have had a knock-on effect on his attitude to all of school," she hesitated. "I know this is down to you and the book club and I just wanted to say thank you and that I'm sorry." She stopped again. "You know, about the not trusting you."

Gabe held his hands up as if to pacify. "Alison, I'm delighted that Robbie is doing so well and I'm really cool about the other stuff. Your job is to make sure Robbie is safe and that's what you did. You're an Ace Mum."

She levered herself to her feet and seemed unsure how to end their conversation and then, unexpectedly, as she was leaving the lift, leant across and gave Gabe a peck on the cheek.

"Well, I just wanted to say 'thank you'."

"Honestly, it has been my pleasure."

Just as he was leaving Gabe said, "Alison, I thought we might have a little party in the lift for Robbie's birthday. I know it's only eighteen days away." He smiled.

Alison laughed. "I know, I get the countdown every morning. I'm taking Robbie and one of his friends to that Tech Alert the weekend before his birthday and then the inevitable MacDonald's. But I haven't got anything planned for his actual birthday, so that would be lovely. I'll have a cake so I'll bring it in."

"Brilliant. I think it will be me and Miss James. Probably Jenny and maybe her mum, and maybe Ginny Cole."

"He'll love it!" Alison left, fluttering one hand as a goodbye. Gabe sat and smiled.

It was much later in the morning that Gabe had a call from the second floor. He knew it had to be Mrs Cole as Mrs Davies had left to drop Jenny off at school, before heading into work, hours ago.

Mrs Cole greeted Gabe with a cheery smile and a "Good morning, Gabe." But she wasn't dressed for the outside. In fact, Gabe noted that she was still wearing her slippers. Fleecy boot types, but definitely slippers. She sat in the armchair, and much as Alison had done earlier, she looked around the lift taking it all in. "Do you know, Gabe, it is so much nicer travelling up and down like this now. It used to be so big and gloomy before."

Gabe smiled and waited. Mrs Cole obviously had something on her mind. Gabe indicated the buttons in a silent question. "Oh, I don't mind. Let's just go up and down."

Gabe pressed the top floor button and sat and waited. The lift creaked into life, and still, Mrs Cole just sat. The lift jolted in place on the third floor, and the doors opened. Gabe pressed for the ground floor and they were on their way again.

"Gabe, can I ask for your opinion on something?"

Gabe shrugged and spread his hands wide.

"It's just that I have plenty of female friends who would give me advice and I think I know what that advice would be, but I wondered if a man's view would be different."

Gabe nodded and appeared to give his consent.

"You know I do my evening class?" Gabe did. Mrs Cole was a great one for classes. Last term she had chosen Beginner's Watercolour classes but had decided, quite early on, that as much as she loved to view paintings, she herself was not a painter. This term it had been Conversational French. She started with the vague idea of reviving any surviving French from her own school days, with a view to perhaps making France a holiday destination in the near future.

"Well, one of my fellow attendees is a rather nice man called Phillip, Phil. He and I have got into the habit of chatting in the coffee break and he's really nice."

*****

Mrs Cole, Ginny, took her cup of coffee over to where Phil was sat reading a flyer. The other members of their group were milling about chatting through mouthfuls of biscuits or replenishing their mugs. Welcoming the break before French verbs were their mission again. Phil looked up as she approached and indicated the chair next to him. He was a good looking man, in that mature way some men are. The greying hair added integrity, and his green/blue eyes showed candour. He wasn't particularly athletic looking. He would say that too many pints down the local had put paid to his shapely figure, but he hadn't let himself go either.

"What's that you've got?" She asked as she sat down. Placing her coffee cup carefully on the table first.

"It's a flyer for that new exhibition space they've opened next to the TIC. Apparently, some of the local art groups are putting on a show from Saturday."

Ginny took the flyer and had a quick read. "Oh, that sounds interesting and something we should support. You know. Local groups."

"Yes. That's what I was thinking." He paused and then rushed, "Would you fancy meeting up and looking at the exhibition together? Perhaps on Monday when it would be quieter."

Ginny paused. She hadn't been out with any man since Graham died. She could hear her friends' voices urging her to say yes, but still, she hesitated.

Believing he'd done the wrong thing Phil tried to cover the awkward moment. "Don't worry if you're busy. It was just an idea."

Mentally she thanked him for the 'get out of jail' card he'd handed her, but instead of using it, she found herself saying, "That would be lovely. How about we go to the coffee shop next door afterwards?"

Phil blew out his cheeks. "That sounds like a plan. What time? Ten thirtyish?"

*****

"I know my girlfriends will say, 'Go for it', but I'm not sure." Mrs Cole looked at Gabe questioningly.

"So, what do you know about him, other than he is taking Conversational French and likes art exhibitions?"

"We've chatted quite a lot. He's a widower. His wife died about fifteen years ago. Like me, he takes classes to keep his brain active and to meet different people. He has a good sense of humour," she trailed off.

"So, if you're friends in class, where's the harm in taking that friendship outside of class?"

"But that's the point. Does he think it's just two friends sharing an interest or does he think this is…well you know, a date?"

"Can't it be both? Don't you want to see where this friendship leads?"

Mrs Cole blushed. "But what happens if he doesn't like me outside the classroom environment? It would be so awkward in class."

"Don't you think he's thought through all that too? I think he was very brave to ask you. I'm not sure I would have done it."

That brought her up short. She hadn't put herself in Phil's position. Yes, it was brave. He had even given her the get-out clause. "I'm being silly, aren't I?"

"No, you're being cautious and that's understandable."

"I also worry that people might think I didn't love Graham. But I did. Moving here was part of coping with his death. I couldn't stay in teaching. It no longer mattered as it used to and I couldn't do that to the children. Graham had been self-employed and hadn't put away the money he said he had, so when it came down to it I had to sell the house to pay off debts. And with no longer having my teacher's salary," again she trailed off.

"When did Graham die?"

"It will be seven years next month."

"Then I think it is time to give the world another go."

"Thank you, Gabe. I just needed to talk it out and get a man's view." She clasped his hands as she waited for the doors to open on her own floor.

Memoir of an Idiot

I don't know if the Lift Book Club is the sort of thing Michael had in mind when he said I should try and improve the residents' life, but it seems to be having that effect. Alison came to see me today and thanked me for helping Robbie. Apparently, his Parents' Evening last night was a great success and Robbie is thriving. I'd forgotten how it feels to be proud of myself. I know it's not just me but to be a part of something so positive is a great feeling.

So, while I'm feeling so positive about myself I'd better look back at Terry. To start with I can't blame it all on Terry. I don't know whether I'd have gone down the same rabbit hole without him but I was my own person and I did these things.

The first thing was that having a skin full the night before was not good for work the next day. My timekeeping went to pot and even when I was there I was in no fit state to work. I also began to miss college. It started with just a few early morning lectures missed but deteriorated into whole days. Mr Bradey took me into his office. He knew Mum was in Manchester and so was really kind, even though he was telling me off. That was my first official warning. It was only a few weeks later that I got my written warning. Mr Bradey spelt it out to me: any continuation in my present behaviour and I would be dismissed. It only took another fortnight.

I didn't tell anyone. Deep down I was so ashamed and yet I couldn't seem to get myself out of this hole I had so willingly jumped into. Mum phoned less frequently but I lied to her about how well I was doing. I didn't tell her that I couldn't sign on because I'd been dismissed and that universal credit was going to take ages before it paid out. She carried on paying my rent and I opted out of evening meals at Mrs G's. I lied, again, and told Mrs G that I was getting my meals at a friend's. She never questioned it, not even when I stopped having breakfast as well.

We weren't allowed to stay in our room during the day and so I began to haunt the college. I had a little money saved and was trying to eke it out. I'd cadge drinks off people, even if I didn't know them very well. It was at the college that Terry caught up with me. I'd been avoiding the pub. Embarrassment and shame again. It was Terry who offered me a job.

Chapter 20
Sam's Story

Sam blew out his breath, pulled back his shoulders and readied himself for what he knew was going to be a very painful and tearful conversation. Although his parents were British born and raised they clung to the African traditions of their ancestors, enforced by their non-British born parents. Sam found these traditions curtailing, especially when overlaid with the religious blackmail of a strict Muslim family. They had been delighted when he said he was going into medicine; outraged that he was going to be a nurse, not a doctor. Now he had to tell them that he was not going to follow their advice about marrying and was, in fact, moving away from home and the city.

It was every bit as painful as he had envisaged. His mother wept and called upon anyone to 'berate her thankless child, Sameer'. His father argued for filial duty and Muslim tradition. But Sam had steeled his heart against them. If he was going to be his own person then he needed to, not only leave the family home but leave the sphere of their influence. He had got a senior nursing post at a hospital on the other side of the country, with the Pennines as his barrier.

Although, when he left home his parents did not resort to 'never darken our door again', neither did they wish him well or help with his move. He was fortunate that the hospital had some accommodation they supplied for as long as he needed it. It was quite close to the hospital and meant he could walk or run to and from work as mood and weather dictated.

Now, stood looking around the tiny flat, he breathed out deeply. His own space. A place to find his own person. It wasn't much and, apart from a beanbag and a suitcase, he had contributed nothing to his new home, but it was bright and sunny; and most importantly of all, it was his and his alone.

Chapter 21

The weather continued to be unseasonal and parents were not looking forward to the half-term holiday due to start in a week. Mr Davies commented to Gabe one morning when once again he'd had to don his overcoat and carry an umbrella. "You may get more customers than you bargained for if news gets around that there's somewhere safe and dry for parents to offload their kiddies to during the holidays."

Gabe pointed to the rules about The Lift Book Club.

"Well, I hope other parents respect that." He sounded like he didn't believe they would for a minute.

Gabe was unsure about Mr Davies. He worked hard, he assumed. Always out by eight in the morning. Often not back before seven in the evening. He wasn't sure what he did exactly. But he assumed the rolled umbrella and briefcase were his signals to the world that he was a man of account. He was a tall man and not particularly broad which gave him a somehow fragile look, not that his face indicated any kind of fragility. Sometimes, Gabe thought, he looked a bit guarded.

The lift doors opened and, as Mr Davies made to leave, he was confronted with a very bedraggled Sam Freedman. "Eh, hello. I didn't realise it was quite that wet out there," said Mr Davies trying to avoid the damp dripping from Sam.

"It's easing off a bit now," Sam breathed. Just a little breathless after his run.

"Right. Cheerio," unfurling his umbrella John Davies headed for the outer doors.

"Sorry, Gabe. I'll stay on the coconut matting or I'm going to drip all over your lovely rug." Sam really appreciated the faded grandeur that Gabe's furnishings had given to the lift space. What little Gabe knew about Sam, he liked. Gabe was unable to divine his heritage. He was a black man of a lithe build and spoke with a slightly northern accent. Gabe thought Yorkshire way but wasn't sure.

Sam nodded towards the rules. "How's the book club coming along?"

"Quite well, really. Robbie, ground floor, Jenny, second floor and Miss James are regular attendees. Although I'm not sure if they'll keep coming once the school holidays start. Mrs Cole, also second floor, has dropped in a few times and made some donations," he pointed to the bookshelf.

"And do you all read the same book or do your own thing?"

"To be honest, it varies. We start off with Robbie reading to me and Jenny to Miss James, but quite often they get involved in whatever Robbie's reading. Or sometimes we all just read our own books."

"Do you know, that sounds blissful? I might come along if you think that's all right?"

Gabe smiled, "As long as you obey the rules," he nodded at the poster, "and you register with Robbie, as the founding member, they would love for others to come along."

"Thanks, Gabe. I might well do that. I have another shift and then I'm off and then back to days. So in a few days' time. Yeh. I might well come along."

He left the lift leaving an obvious damp patch on the matting and squelched his way along the corridor to his flat.

Memoir of an Idiot

Its Robbie's birthday tomorrow and we're going to have a little party in the lift. I know it sounds silly but I'm really looking forward to it. It feels good to be doing something nice for someone. Although I'm not sure how the blancmange rabbit and jelly will go down with Robbie. He might think it's babyish. I think its good fun.

Sam also said he might come along to the book club. It would be good if he does. Show Robbie that fit young men read as well. That it's not a nerdy thing to do. I know Robbie likes it at the moment but he's coming to that age when he needs good male role models. Perhaps that was my problem. After Dad died, I didn't have many male role models. There were the teachers at school and I really looked up to Mr Bradey but I'm not sure if I accepted them as role models. Mind you I can't say I thought Terry was a good role model but it's his lead I followed.

Terry introduced me to Daz. No idea, even now, of what his real name is. Daz needed couriers. People to take his drugs to his dealers around the town. They had to be unknown to the police, 'off the plod's radar' is how Daz explained it. Every trip was £50. Fifty pounds to walk across town making drops. I'd like to say that I said no at first but I didn't. When you're eating from the supermarkets' whoopsie counter and cadging drinks from anyone, £50 was treasure.

And it was easy. Once I got over the first panic that every passing police car was after me. No seedy alleyways or dead of night meets: my 'customers' were a lot like Terry, amiable, cheerful and looked respectable. I'd like to say I'd learnt my lesson from getting sacked and never touched a drop of alcohol again but I didn't. As soon as I had money in my pocket I was at the bar. I ate better but I drank more.

Chapter 22

Before Sam could attend the book club, it was Robbie's party. Gabe had enlisted the help of Miss James, who had volunteered to make the sandwiches. Gabe invested in some paper plates and spoons and Kathy Davies had volunteered to make jelly and blancmange in a rabbit mould. She wouldn't come to the party but Jenny would be there.

The day of the party Miss James carefully wheeled her hostess trolley into the lift. Sandwiches on the top and plates of biscuits underneath. The next stop was floor two for Jenny and the rabbit mould. Kathy was waiting, proudly holding a silver platter with a pink blancmange rabbit tucking into green jelly. Gabe thought it looked rather good and Miss James said, "I haven't seen one of those since I was a girl. How wonderful!"

Jenny danced about her mother, "I chopped up the jelly. He's eating the jelly, isn't he?"

"He is. It looks great," said Gabe. He placed the platter royally on the half-moon table.

On the ground floor, Robbie was waiting. He looked stunned for a second and then laughed. "Is this my birthday party? For me?"

At that moment his mum appeared behind him holding a cake with nine lit candles on. She began to sing, "Happy birthday to you," The others joined in. Robbie looked a little red-faced but was grinning from ear to ear. At the conclusion of the song, Alison lowered the cake and Robbie blew out the candles. The occupants of the lift cheered.

Alison stayed with the book club for the party making use of one of Miss James' spare chairs. She and Miss James talked together. Gabe didn't catch all of what they were talking about, but it seemed Alison was thanking Miss James for becoming a surrogate grandma for Robbie. Gabe heard. "I don't see my own mum now, but I remember, as a girl, how important it was for me to have grandparents to go to."

Miss James pattered her hand. "It's a pleasure and an honour. He's such a likeable young man. You should be very proud of him and yourself."

Alison smiled and blushed. To hide her embarrassment she called, "Robbie, how many helpings of blancmange is that?"

Robbie smiled sheepishly. "Only my third!"

The company laughed.

Chapter 23

True to his word Sam attended The Lift Book Club a few days later. He carried a book in one hand and a large beanbag in the other. He addressed himself to Robbie. "May I join The Lift Book Club, please? My name is Sam and I live in flat 5."

"Hello, Sam," said Miss James. "How lovely of you to join us. Robbie do you want to write Sam's name in the register?"

"Okay. How do you spell Sam?"

Sam sounded out the letters and then placed his beanbag in the corner by the bookshelf.

"Where you from. Sam? You talk funny?"

"Nay, lad. Thou talks funny," Sam did his best mimicry of a Yorkshire man. Gabe and Miss James laughed.

"I don't talk funny!" Robbie said indignantly.

Gabe said, trying to placate Robbie's outrage. "Everyone has an accent, the way their words sound and it depends on where they come from. Sam didn't grow up in Swanton," Gabe checked this with Sam, who nodded, "so he doesn't sound like you: he has a different accent. If you went to where Sam grew up everyone would sound like him and you would sound like you talked funny."

"But you don't talk as funny as Sam and you're not from Swanton," queried Robbie.

"True, but you've noticed that I don't sound exactly like you do, so I have an accent as well."

"And sometimes you can change your accent," added Miss James. "When I worked for Mr Etherington and I needed to make a telephone call to someone important," and here she broke into RP, rounding her vowels, "I would talk like this."

"My mum does that on the phone sometimes, if she has to talk to the people at work." Light dawning on Robbie's face. But then he turned back to Sam and said, "But where are you really from?"

"Robbie!" Gabe said warningly, but Sam held up his hand. "Do you mean that because I am black I must be from another country?"

Robbie considered, "Well, yeh. Or are your mum and dad from somewhere else?"

"My parents were both born in Britain. My father in London and my mum in Leeds, which is also in Yorkshire. But my grandparents all come from the continent of Africa, but four different parts of Africa."

*****

"Sameer! It is you. Come in! Come in!" Aunty Gladys flung her door wide and hugged Sameer hard before pulling him in. "Let me have a look at you." She held him at arm's length and stared hard at his face.

"You have your grandma's cheekbones, that's for sure. Your eyes are your Mums and she got them from her dad, your Pappy. The rest of you must come from your dad's side of the family."

And when he was with Dad's relative it would be: "You got that beautiful hair from your Gran and that nose could only be from your Grandpa."

Sam always felt that he was like a police e-fit. His face was a composite of his inheritance. It was part of the reason he moved away from his family. He wanted to be Sam Freedman. His own person.

*****

"If you had a map I could show you. My grandparents come from Morocco, Ghana, Madagascar and Egypt."

"Is Egypt in Africa?" Robbie queried. "We did a project on the pyramids and stuff. They don't look like Africans."

"Africa is a big continent, made up of thirty or forty different countries, so there are a lot of different types of people. Not just negroes."

Robbie contemplated that for a few seconds and then gave the non-committal response, "Okay."

Inquisition over everyone got down to their respective books. Robbie was still on the Harry Potter and soon all of them were listening to his reading.

Memoir of an Idiot

I've had an idea. I want to buy Robbie one of those map books for children. The ones that show lots of information about the country, sort of a bit like a cartoon. We had one in school, in the Geography class. So I've spoken with Pat about needing to speak with Michael. I'd expected it would be a few days before I heard back but later this evening there was a knock at the door and there was Michael.

"Good timing, my boy. I was in Swanton on another matter when Pat contacted me. How are you doing? How's the work coming along?"

I tried to explain about the nomadic room and The Lift Book Club. I'm not sure if he really understood what I was talking about but he clapped his hands together in glee. "My, my! What an unusual turn of events. Very enterprising of you, my boy."

I tried to tell him that it was Miss James' idea and that it was just a way of trying to help Robbie but he said, "Yes, but from that one good turn, look what has developed. Now, sorry to rush you. But I have to be away soon. What did you want to talk to me about?"

I explained about the atlas and how today Sam was talking about where his family is from and that I thought one of those children's atlases, the ones where they also give information about the people, the language, that sort of thing, would be a good present.

He asked me how much I would need. I didn't have a clue. I don't think I've ever bought a new book in my life. My books are either from the library or the charity shops.

Michael contemplated the corner of the room and I thought he was going to refuse. I told him I hadn't been anywhere near drugs. I think I sounded desperate too.

Michael refocused his gaze on me and said, "No, no, my dear boy. Just trying to remember the cost of books these days. I think you will find something good is going to cost at least £20, so if I give you £30, you should be covered." He rummaged in his trouser pocket. Then removed his hand and tapped at his chest and grinned. "Wallet!"

He took out his wallet and handed me three £10 notes and said. "You may keep the change. Now I must be off. Good luck young man. You're making a fine show of it." With that, he left, closing the door softly behind him.

Chapter 24

The following day, after the workers had left, Gabe knocked at Mrs Cole's, Miss James' and Captain Clive's flat to explain that he was going out in his lunch break and so the lift would be self-service for about an hour.

Mrs Cole said. "Don't worry, Gabe. I'm off out at ten. I'm meeting Phil for the exhibition viewing." She smiled, perhaps nervously.

"Thank you, Gabe. I won't be out and about today. The wind is from the East," said Miss James.

"Right you are," said Captain Clive. "Not off out until tomorrow. Seventeen hundred hours. Comrades' Club."

Mrs Cole did go out at ten. She did look nervous, Gabe decided. She was banking on the dry, if windy day, and had on a short suede jacket in tan and a cream-coloured pleated skirt that swirled as she walked.

"You look lovely," said Gabe.

"Thank you, Gabe."

They stood in silence as the lift faltered down to the ground floor. As she left she said, "Wish me luck."

"No luck needed. Just enjoy the company."

As promised Gabe was only out for the hour and returned with a large flat box under one arm. He placed it next to the half-moon table and smiled to himself.

Mid-afternoon Mrs Cole arrived back. She was smiling broadly. "You were right, Gabe. No luck needed. I have had a lovely time. Phil is quite knowledgeable about painting styles and we have similar tastes in what we like. I was worried that we would run out of things to say, but we didn't. In fact, we said our goodbyes and then spent several more minutes talking about the play the local Amdram group is putting on and we're going to go and see it." There was a breathless quality to her speech.

Gabe smiled in reply. "Perhaps you could go for a quick bite before the show?"

"Now, there's an idea. It's our last class this week so I'll ask him. We could try that little Chinese by St Peter's. It's supposed to be nice in there."

When Mrs Cole got out on the second floor Gabe wasn't sure but he thought he saw a little skip from her as she left the lift.

The Lift Book Club assembled at its usual time that evening. Jenny Davies had a new book that her Grandma had sent her and was eager to read it to Miss James. Sam came, with his bean bag again and Robbie had his last school book of the term. He was keen to finish it and did within twenty minutes.

"Well done, Robbo. You have really got your reading sussed," said Gabe.

Robbie smiled and said confidingly, "I didn't realise books could be fun!"

Gabe leant down to the flat box he had brought in at lunchtime. He handed it to Robbie and said, "I have been so impressed with your reading and what your teacher said at parents' evening that I thought you deserved a present."

Robbie's mouth fell open. "For me? Really?"

"Yeh. Sorry, it's not wrapped."

Robbie opened the box and pulled out a large book. About the size of a tabloid newspaper, entitled Maps.

"Wow!" was the only word Robbie could summon.

"It was Sam who gave me the idea. You can look and see where Egypt is in Africa and the other countries his grandparents come from."

"Oh, wow!" Robbie repeated. He hadn't yet opened the book but just kept staring at the front cover.

"Okay, Robbie. If you bring it over here I can show you where my family comes from," said Sam.

Robbie cradled the large book and took it to Sam. He squatted next to him on the beanbag. Sam shuffled one way a little to make room. Reverentially Robbie laid the book on his lap and opened to the inside cover where a map of the world showed the countries covered in the book and on which pages to find them.

Sam pointed. "See, all that is Africa and there is Egypt" his finger moved down the page, "and that island, there. That's Madagascar, that's where my mum's dad comes from." His finger moved again. This time across the page, "And over this side is my dad's parents. Ghana is here," he tapped on the page, "and then this is Morocco. Shall we look at the pages about them? If you already know about Egypt which other one do you want to see?"

"Madagascar. There's a cartoon film about that. But I didn't know it was a real place."

There was a rustle of pages and Robbie flicked through. "Number 74," he said to himself and then stopped at the relevant page. He and Sam bent their heads over the pages but had to turn the book on its side to see the island laid out across the double page. Quiet murmurings took the pair of them around the island.

Gabe glanced over to Miss James who smiled and nodded. At the end of the session, Robbie looked a bit troubled.

"What's the matter, Robbo?"

"Do I have to sign this book out on the Loans page?"

"No, Robbie. That book is yours. It is a present. You take it home with you."

Clutching the book Robbie ran from the lift, already calling for his mum.

Chapter 25
Captain Roger Clive's Story

"No, I'm sorry, Roger, but I don't want you having anything more to do with James."

Roger Clive sat in his chair, shell shocked, but not about to show this damn woman how hard it had hit him. "Right. James is to have nothing more to do with me? His uncle? His only uncle on his father's side?"

She paced around the room, occasionally disappearing behind his chair, but he refused to turn around and follow her. "Yes. I know you have been very good to him. To both of us. But you fill his head with such nonsense about how good a life on the sea is and it isn't. Look what it did for George."

"Any job has risks. Die at sea. Die under a car."

"Yes, but the sea is a much bigger risk. Come on, Roger, you know that."

"If that is what you wish? I will abide by your decision. How will you explain it to the boy?"

"You go away to sea. He'll just accept that. In time, he'll forget. I really am sorry, Roger."

Roger ignored the sentiment. "What about his school?"

"Well, of course, I shan't expect you to continue to contribute. If needs be, he can go to the local school."

Roger shook his head. "I will continue to pay his fees. Told George I would look out for you both."

"No, you can't do that, Roger."

"I can. I will. It's for the boy, not for you."

And so Captain Roger Clive lost his only remaining relative. A loss that bit deep into his soul, but he wasn't about to go against Jane's wishes. He'd keep track of the boy, long distance.

For the next eleven years, he paid for his nephew's schooling; boarding school, university. Then came a call.

"Hello, is that Captain Clive? Captain Roger Clive?"

"Yes. To whom am I speaking?"

"This is James Clive. I don't know if you remember me?"

"Of course, I do my boy. How lovely to hear from you. How are you?" His throat tightened with emotion.

"Oh, I'm fine. I've had a long chat with Mum and I know all about her asking you not to see me and you still paying for my education. And I wanted to thank you, sincerely, for doing that."

Captain Clive cleared his throat and wiped at his eyes. "I promised your father I would look out for you."

"Well, I think you are amazing, especially after Mum banned you from my life."

"How is your Mother?"

"Oh, all right. Well, really a bit upset. Partly because we have had a bit of a row about how badly she treated you, but also because I'm going on a trek in Tanzania. I'm part of a group looking at the primates in the forests." Passion entered his voice. "Do you know hundreds of thousands of acres of forest have been destroyed this year alone?"

"No. So you are going to do what. Exactly?"

"I'm part of a team going to record where the primates are, which species and how the destruction is impacting on their ecosystems." Now his voice sounded a bit embarrassed, "It's partly the reason I got in touch. You see I need some money to pay my share of the costs. That's how I found out about you. I went to Mum for a loan, thinking she had some resources and found out it was all up to you."

Long after the call finished Captain Clive sat looking out of his window. He liked his third floor flat. He had views across Old Swanton. A view of the canal, which could be nicer, but it was moving water. He was content enough. He read a lot. Cooked well for himself. Visited the Old Comrades Club once a month. But it would be nice to have his nephew back in his life.

So what about the money he wanted? The boy talked about paying it back. Being an eco-warrior was not going to earn him big money so it well may be he would never see it again. He had his nest egg from his retirement. What was he planning to do with it? Well, his funeral was one consideration. Other than that, rainy day contingency. His flat was paid for. He had his pension for everyday needs. What rainy day could he expect? None came to mind. The money was sent to James. He had one postcard when they arrived in Tanzania, but after that radio silence as they were in the bush for most of their work.

"You killed him," the words sobbed out of the telephone receiver.

"What?"

"He's dead!"

Captain Clive recognised the clogged voice. 'He' could only mean James.

"What's happened? Stop crying and tell me." His voice was strident with urgency.

"His group was set upon by locals. They objected to the survey they were trying to carry out. It happened at night. Three have been killed and…" She wailed. "They killed my boy."

He was stuck for words, "I…"

"I told you to stay away from him. You were the danger. You killed him." The phone went dead.

Captain Clive starred at it long after the call had finished. Dreams of afternoon's chatting with James dispersed in the misery that swelled inside him. And the guilt. Searing, piercing guilt making it difficult for him to breathe. "The road to hell is paved with good intentions," he murmured to himself. How wrong he had been. Suddenly the future took on a greyer hue.

Chapter 26

The next day Robbie returned to The Lift Book Club with his new book and an envelope. In his neatest writing, he had addressed the envelope to Gabe. Inside was a homemade 'Thank you' card. Gabe was delighted. He realised it was probably the most precious thing anyone had given him in a long time.

Robbie was keen to continue to explore the world. He looked at the world map and then decided on a destination. Tonight he wanted to look at the other places Sam had mentioned, even though Sam wasn't there because he was back on nights.

Robbie had read about Ghana and was just about to start on Morocco when a call came for the third floor. Gabe knew that would be Captain Clive off out for his social at the Comrades Club.

Captain Clive looked every bit the retired naval man. His grey beard was cut close to his face and his hair was the old fashioned, 'short back and sides'. He was wearing a dark blue blazer, complete with medals, a white shirt and the Comrades Club tie. His fawn trousers were pressed razor sharp and highly polished shoes finished the ensemble.

"Ah. The Book Club. Yes, saw the notice. What are you reading, young man?" He addressed Robbie in this brisk manner.

Robbie was a little in awe of the Captain. "A map book, sir."

"Now that looks like a good read." He came and stood next to Robbie and leant over to have a closer look. At this point, Robbie was still on the world map page. "Ah, yes," the Captain pointed. "Been there. And there. Oh, we had a fun time there." His fingered stabbed and moved around the pages.

He looked up and said to Gabe. "Been around the world more times than I can remember. Stories from every port."

On impulse Gabe said. "Perhaps you would like to join our book club and talk to us about the different ports and countries you've visited, sir."

"What?" The Captain was obviously surprised by the invitation. "You here every evening?"

"Just weekdays," said Robbie, "and we come after tea at half-past four and finish…when we finish."

"Yes our finishing time is a bit fluid," admitted Gabe, "but you can come for as long or as short a time as you wish. We have plenty of chairs."

"Umh. Think about it." With that, the doors of the lift opened onto the ground floor and the Captain strode across the foyer.

The book club continued its reading.

Later that evening the Captain returned. Still as smart as when he went out. A little flushed in the cheeks but steady on his feet. "Ah, Gabe. Glad you're still here." The Captain didn't know that most nights Gabe stayed on until all the residents were home.

"Thought about your idea. Might well join you. No experience of children. Too many days at sea for family."

"I am sure everyone would love to hear your tales from the places you've visited, Captain. Robbie is fascinated by his map book and the countries he's learning about. I think he would be overjoyed to hear from someone who's actually visited them."

The Captain stepped out on the third floor. "Might see you Wednesday. Good night, Gabe."

The Captain turned to his flat and took out his keys. Gabe waited until he had gone in and closed the door. It would be nice to see the Captain at the book club, he thought.

Chapter 27

Captain Roger Clive's Story

He rushed down the gangplank as soon as they were given shore leave. He sped out the dock gates and headed for the florist, who always had a good supply of flowers in when a ship was due. He was ahead of the pack and soon had a glorious bunch of spring flowers in his hand. He debated whether to walk or catch the next bus, but a bus pulled in as he stood there and that made his mind up.

Upstairs, on the number twenty-two, he looked down on all the familiar landmarks. The old swimming baths. Due to be closed. Past The Royal, Portsmouth's oldest hospital. Charles Dickens lived just across the way for a short time because his dad worked in the Dockyard. Anticipation beat in his chest. He'd been debating all this last trip whether or not to ask Rosie to marry him, and he had decided he would. At this time of the day, she'd be just finishing work at the local library. She was a cut above the other girls he knew. She'd stayed on at school and got her GCE Certificates and then applied as a trainee in the library. That was the kind of girl he wanted as a wife.

Outside Rosie's home, he straightened his cap and brushed down his uniform. He took a deep breath and knocked at the door. It was a nice area, Cosham. Her dad was the office manager at Brytree & Sons, the local solicitors. Every house had a little front garden. Just enough to show off a few good plants and a bush or two.

The door opened and Rosie's mum stood there. "Roger Clive! Home on shore leave? How are your mum and dad?"

"Evening Mrs Rodgers, um is Rosie in? I haven't seen Mum and Dad yet, but last time they wrote they were fine."

"Come in. I'll give Rosie a call." He entered and shut the door behind him and Mrs Rodgers leant up the stairs and called "Rosie! Roger Clive is here."

She turned back to him, "She won't be long. Do you want to wait here or come into the back?"

"I'll wait here if that's all right?"

She nodded and walked into the kitchen. Carefully closing the door behind her. She had been unable to miss the brightly coloured flowers in his hands. She hoped her Rosie knew what she was doing.

Rosie came down the stairs slowly. Roger beamed as she came into view. Long dark hair, curled at the ends. A pale blue frock gathered at the waist and flared out to calf length. She looked beautiful. Every bit the dream girl he had held in his heart these last four months.

"Hello, Rosie. These are for you," thrusting the flowers into her hands.

"Oh, thanks, Roger. You home on leave?" Her expression wasn't as welcoming as he had expected. Just surprised, probably.

"Yes. We got in about lunchtime and given leave about an hour ago and I came straight here. How are you, Rosie?" He went to take her hand, but she moved away.

"I better put these in water. They're lovely Roger, but you shouldn't be spending your money on me."

"Of course, I should. How've you been keeping, Rosie?" He sidestepped nervously as Rosie moved towards the kitchen door. "Do you want to come for a walk? It's still a lovely evening out."

"Sorry, Roger, I can't. I'm expecting someone."

"Oh, right. I should have realised you would have plans. I didn't think. Is it someone who would understand that you'd want to spend time with me after I've been away for so long?"

There was a moment's hesitation before she said, "It's lovely to see you Roger but I'm seeing someone else," her eyes were cast down.

An arrow split his heart. He knew it had to be an arrow; the pain was so sharp. The air left his body. He felt himself wilt, only willpower kept him upright. He managed, "Someone else?"

"Yes." Now she raised her gaze. "Look, Roger. You're a lovely boy and fun to be with, but I want someone who's going to be here for me."

"But I am here for you. I'd do anything for you, you know that." His clearly imagined marriage proposal was dying in front of his eyes.

"But you're not here, Roger. Not for months at a time, you're not here. I want someone who comes home every night. You can't expect someone to wait every time you go off to sea."

"But… Women do wait. Chaps on board are married."

"Yes. But do they know what their wives get up to when they're away? I could tell you stories that would make your hair curl!" She was getting angry now. She had tried to be reasonable, but he wasn't listening.

He felt sick. He needed to leave. This wasn't the Rosie who had stolen his heart. Had he made her up? Was he wrong to expect her to wait? Could he give up the sea? He fumbled for the door latch and stepped out. Without a backward glance, he left. He would never trust his heart again.

Memoir of an idiot

Robbie loves his Map book. He and Sam have been visiting all the countries connected with Sam's family. We might also get the Captain to come and talk about some of the places. He seemed very interested in what Robbie was reading. I'm sure a bit of company would do him some good. I don't think he sees anyone to talk to apart from me on a Friday morning, his visits to the library and his Comrades' Club buddies. I do hope he comes.

I've been putting off writing down the next part of my story. Not that it hasn't been whirling around my head for the last few days. Hopefully, if I put it down on paper it will stop haunting me.

I became a regular courier for Daz. I knew it was wrong. I knew I should get a proper job but, if I'm honest, Daz' job was easier and paid a lot more than any real job I would get. The visits to the pub continued, but somehow it had lost its pleasure. I didn't get that high when you're out enjoying yourself. I wasn't enjoying myself. Just drinking in the pub was better than sitting in my room at Mrs G's.

So one night I'm sat in the pub feeling, to say 'down' would be an understatement, I was at my lowest, and in walks Terry. I hadn't seen him in a while. He sees that I'm low and suggests a quick snort. This shows you how naive I was, I didn't have a clue what he was on about. Of course, he meant smack, heroin.

Chapter 28

Gabe had been unsure whether Robbie would want to continue with The Lift Book Club once the summer holidays began, but he did. With no family locally to share child care, Alison had booked Robbie into a Holiday Play Scheme. "Like school, but more running about," had been Robbie's verdict. And so The Lift Book Club continued as before.

It was a few days before Captain Clive joined them. Despite the summer heat, the weather had decided to co-operate with the parents' need for a dry spell, he was wearing a shirt and tie and a knitted jumper.

Gabe gave him the Captain's chair, "Only appropriate don't you think, sir?" he smiled, as he got out one of Miss James' folding chairs. "Robbie do you want to show the Captain your Map book, perhaps he can tell you more about some of the countries."

Robbie was still bewitched by the Map book and eager to share it with anyone. "I've looked at Madagascar, Ghana and Morocco coz that's where Sam's grandparents come from; and Egypt, but I know about pharaohs and things."

"Did you know they eat camel in Morocco? I had camel meatballs once. Quite tasty."

Robbie looked at him round-eyed. "They eat camel?"

"Certainly do. In fact, they use up everything a camel produces. When alive they milk it. Like a cow. They use the dung for their fires, once it's dried. They eat the meat. What do you think they do with the hump, eh?"

"Isn't the hump full of water?"

"No. It's a sack of fat. They use it for cooking. Like lard?"

Robbie looked unsure.

"Perhaps your mum uses cooking oil," Gabe suggested. "So the people of Morocco use the camel's fat hump to melt and use in cooking." He checked with the Captain who nodded.

"Had a three-day stopover in Tangier, Can you find it on the map, boy?"

101

Robbie looked at the map. If the Captain was a sailor Tangier would be on the coast. He found it and pointed.

"Good man."

*****

The sound of the call to prayer wafted across the harbour. They were having an enforced stopover in Tangier due to needing a part for the engine. The First Mate had it all under control with a skeleton crew on board. Everyone else was on leave, including him.

He strolled through the streets of the town. The Mediterranean style merging seamlessly with the Arabic. In places, there was a touch of the African, but mainly this was an Arab town. He had picked up a guidebook and read about Tangier's place in the trade routes up from the Sahara and West Africa through to Europe. Gold, leather, ivory, salt and slaves. He was surprised to hear about the slaves, but apparently, many of the African tribes sold their enemies into slavery. The guidebook recommended a trip to the city of Fez and its ninth-century walled city, still only accessible to pedestrians and donkeys. Getting there proved to be an experience in its self. Sleek, if old fashioned, Mercedes taxis queued in a square. He had managed to find a taxi going to Fez; he then had to negotiate a price. Fortunately, for him, an English speaking merchant joined in the discussion and explained that the fare would be divided by as many passengers as there were in the car.

His co-passenger, Abasi, explained some of the sites they passed until they reached the open countryside. Then he talked about his business. He was going to Fez to buy leather goods. Fez had been tanning and making leather since the tenth century. Beautiful workmanship.

Twice on the journey, they stopped to pick up other passengers. He had expected the fourth passenger to sit in the front, especially as he had a live chicken, with its feet tied, hung over one shoulder. But no. Everyone piled into the back seat.

Fez and the walled city were worth the journey. Abasi kindly directed him to a cheap and clean 'caravanserai'. Apparently, in the days of the trading caravans along the salt roads, these were the places to stop. The lower space, he was told, had once been stables and warehouses. Now they were workshops and selling spaces. Above were rooms, and food was served.

He loved the walled city. Narrow streets and windy stepped lanes. He felt no threat. Everyone smiled and nodded. The city was totally untouched by modern life. He heard nothing that would not have been heard several hundreds of years ago. A revolting smell led him to the tannery. An enormous area of stone baths filled with noxious substances. Racks of leather drying in the sun. Men sat outside workshops, tools in hand shaping leather into bags, wallets, belts and more.

Tired he returned to the caravanserai and ate the meatballs, only later finding out that they were camel. In the market, he had seen a camel meat seller, complete with camel head hanging outside the stall and the camel's fat hump swaying above the butcher's head. He'd passed, what he assumed was a baker's, and was tantalised by the smell of warm bread.

The following day he spent a short while looking at Fez University. Apparently, it had been set up in the ninth century and by a woman. It was still one of the most remarkable buildings in the city. All too soon it was time to negotiate his return journey to Tangier. A squashed, if uneventful time.

Chapter 29

Everyone had been enthralled by the Captain's tale, but Gabe could see that the memory had been a tiring experience for him. It wasn't until several days later that Gabe saw the Captain again.

"Good evening at your book club, Gabe."

"I'm glad you enjoyed it, Captain. They're a good crowd and they were fascinated by your story. Perhaps you would come again and tell us more?"

"Yes. Like to do that. Bright youngster, the boy."

"Yes, he is. Just needs a bit of encouragement."

"Probably see you Wednesday. Quiet day, Wednesdays."

True to his word the Captain appeared on Wednesday and every Wednesday for the next few months. Using Robbie's book The Lift Book Club visited the world, highlighted by stories of the Captain's forty-six years of adventure. There seemed to be no corner of the world that the Captain had not visited at least once, and many that he had seen several times. Robbie was round-eyed with excitement every time. Gabe was sure that at some point Robbie might announce his intention of becoming a sailor.

One day they had been talking about Madagascar. The Captain had made a visit long before Robbie had been born. "Lovely people, the Malagasy," the Captain had mused.

"Is Madagascar anything like what they show in the film?" Robbie queried. "What film is that?"

"You know, Madagascar. It's a film about animals escaping from a zoo and going to find Madagascar. I just wanted to know whether it really was like that."

"Sorry. Not a film I know."

"I've got the DVD if you want to see it. You can borrow it," Robbie encouraged.

"Um, well. I do have a DVD player but I find it difficult to read the buttons. Don't know which ones to press."

"Oh, I can do that," said Robbie nonchalantly. "I can come and set it up if you want." He looked at the Captain enquiringly. Gabe wasn't sure whether to intervene but one look at the sparkle in Miss James' eyes kept him quiet.

"Well, that's very good of you, Robbie. Thank you. I would like to watch your DVD."

At this point, Gabe did intervene. "You better check with your mum, first. Robbie."

"Oh, she won't mind."

Miss James sensed Gabe's unease and addressed the Captain. "I hope you don't think I am being overly familiar, but could I join you to watch this film? I don't have a DVD player."

"My dear lady, of course. I will get some biscuits in. Or it should it be popcorn?" he chuckled. "Right check which day would be best for your mum, Robbie and we will have a film show."

"We could have a Film Club as well as a book club," enthused Robbie, "cool!"

*****

It had been decided that Sunday afternoon was a good time to hold the Film Club. Both Alison and Miss James joined Robbie and the Captain. Robbie had brought his Madagascar DVD, Alison a cake and Miss James some biscuits. The Captain welcomed them into his home. The flat was sparse but spick and span. Framed photographs of ships and crews, the Captain had served on and with, lined the walls. A bookshelf at one end saw books neatly placed in alphabetical order. The Captain had placed two armchairs and a wicker one in a half-circle in front of the television. "Make yourselves comfortable, ladies. I'll just pop your thoughtful gifts into the kitchen."

When he returned he pointed to a square leather type box to Robbie, "You can have the tuffet. Bring it over between the two chairs."

Robbie was surprised at how heavy it was, and how solid when he sat on it. The Captain pointed to the television and DVD and said, "All yours, my boy."

Robbie knelt in front of them both. The remote controls were both sat on the side. Robbie turned on the television and then the DVD. The eject drawer opened and he placed his DVD in and closed it again. Everyone could hear the whirring.

"Yes, I can get that far," said the Captain, "but I can't get it to come on the television."

Robbie looked at the television remote and pressed a button. The screen came alive with adverts from Robbie's DVD. "Show me which button," said the Captain. Robbie went over and explained which button to use and how to get the television back to programme mode. Having got the technicalities sorted they settled back for the big attraction!

Alison was pleased to see that both Miss James and the Captain seemed to be enjoying the cartoon nonsense. The Captain guffawed a few times and Miss James tapped her fingers to the beat of the music. Perhaps a Film Club was a possibility.

Memoir of an Idiot

The residents have started a Film Club. It's being held in the Captain's flat, normally on a Sunday afternoon. I think it's brilliant. Robbie tells me which films he is taking up and then all about them on the way down. His mum goes as well, sometimes and I think Miss James goes every week.

It made me smile and think about my own childhood. Me and Gran spent a lot of time together and one of our favourite things was watching old movies together. We'd both be on the sofa, at each end, and she'd have her feet on my lap. A blanket over both of us and a packet of sweets in the middle. The number of old films we saw together. All the musicals of the forties and fifties. Gran would sing along and tap her feet against my thighs. Even now it makes me smile even if there is also a pang of regret for magic times lost.

I thought the heroin was going to give me some magic times. The first time I tried it I wasn't sure I liked the effect. It made me feel sick and sleepy. Terry said that was because I had been drinking. Try it when you're sober. You'll love it. I did. Terry said Daz only ever cut his heroin with powdered milk so he was a 'safe' dealer. Terry gave me my first and second hit as 'gifts', but after that, I had to pay. The price was £10 a bag. At first, that was fine, but the euphoric sensations became shorter and the itch to take more got stronger and so I needed more. But I had a job so that was okay. That was until Daz found out I was a user. He wasn't happy. Users were unreliable, he said. And there was always the temptation of dipping into the stock. Not me, I said but he wouldn't listen.

So now I had a drug problem that I couldn't support, even with the social coming in each month.

Chapter 30

The Harrington Hall Film Club became another regular feature of life. Normally on a Sunday afternoon, sometimes on a Saturday. It turned out that Captain Clive was quite a film fan and had a collection of DVDs, but couldn't work the player. He and Robbie came to a mutual agreement that they alternate Robbie's film collection with his own. Robbie did explain to Gabe that some of the films were very, very old, but quite interesting, sometimes.

Jenny didn't join the Film Club, but Miss James was a regular member. The times Miss James couldn't make it Alison would go along. She did confide in Gabe. "It's nice for Robbie. He hasn't got any grandparents and these are good role models for him." Gabe noticed that Alison also seemed to benefit from the Film Club. She seemed more relaxed and content when she travelled down from a screening of the latest choice. Gabe also discovered that Miss James and the Captain took their adoptive grandparenting roles very seriously. He didn't know how the discussion had come about but one Sunday afternoon after the film club Robbie informed Gabe that he wasn't going to the Holiday Play Scheme every day for the rest of the holiday, "Miss James and the Captain are going to take me out or let me be in their flats."

And so it transpired for the rest of Robbie's holiday he spent three days in the play scheme and two days with Miss James and the Captain. If the weather was dry they took strolls to the town, visiting the little museum, the art exhibition space as well as the swings and roundabouts.

Miss James confided to Gabe one afternoon when she and Robbie had gone together to the museum. "He's a lovely boy and so bright. I wasn't sure he'd like the museum, but this is the second time we've been there."

"I think you're right. He is a very curious child. I was delighted with his response to the map book I bought him."

Miss James nodded. "I know the Captain is delighted at that interest." She leant forward conspiratorially, "I think he missed having someone to tell his stories to."

Gabe nodded and Miss James continued. "He was saying only the other day that Robbie makes him feel twenty years younger," she paused, "and if I'm honest. He's given me something new to think about."

Chapter 31

All too soon, for Robbie, at least, it was the new term. The day before Robbie had sought Gabe out. "Gabe, its school tomorrow."

"I know. Have you got your school uniform sorted?"

Robbie nodded. Gabe sensed there was something else going on. "Are you looking forward to it?"

Robbie twisted the cuff of one of his sleeves. "Sort of."

"Anything worrying you? New teacher?" Gabe said insightfully.

"Yeh. It's Mr Groves."

"What's he like?"

"I've heard him shout a lot. And kids say he's really, really, strict. They say he says he only wants 100% effort."

"That's okay, isn't it? You've been brilliant at school. You like it and you are good at it."

"But what if he don't like me?"

"Doesn't like me. Not don't. But why shouldn't he like you?"

"I dunno. Mrs Hart didn't like me."

"Robbie!" Gabe exclaimed. "That is just plain untrue. Mrs Hart wrote a wonderful report about you and you got two certificates from her. Of course she liked you."

Ignoring this truth Robbie continued, "And what if the works too hard?"

"I'd be surprised if it wasn't harder than the work in Mrs Hart's class because you've gone up a year. But it won't be too hard. Just remember how difficult you found reading this time last year. Now, look at you. Reading Harry Potter all by yourself."

Having had all his arguments effectively wiped out Robbie whispered, with tears threatening on the rims of his eyes. "I'm just scared."

"Oh, Robbo. There's nothing to be scared of." Gabe put his hands on Robbie's shoulders but avoided a hug. He looked into Robbie's eyes and gently shook him. "You know the school, this is just a new teacher. You did the scariest thing the first day you ever went to school."

Robbie didn't look convinced.

"What is the worst thing that could go wrong?"

Robbie shrugged his shoulders and wouldn't make eye contact.

"Look. I tell you what," said Gabe reaching into the inside of his shirt. "I'll let you have my lucky white feather." He passed Robbie a small fluffy feather and laid it gently in his hand.

Robbie stared at it. It was soft and slightly shimmery. "Are you sure, Gabe? Won't you need it?"

"You can borrow it for tomorrow, how's that?"

"Thanks, Gabe." He gave him an unexpected hug and closing his fist tightly over the feather left the lift.

Chapter 32

Gabe was waiting by the lift to see Robbie off the next morning. They didn't exchange words, but Robbie tapped his shirt pocket and Gabe gave him the thumbs up. It was also Jenny's first day at 'big school' and she couldn't sit still for excitement.

Mrs Davies looked a bit tearful. "I can't believe she's school age already."

"I'm a big girl now," Jenny proclaimed.

"You certainly are," said Gabe. "You look like a big school girl in your uniform."

"She's just going for the morning today and tomorrow and then she'll stay and have lunch and then its whole days. They're very good there." Gabe thought Mrs Davies was trying to convince herself more than him or Jenny.

"I've been in my big class, lots of times." With the emphasis on 'lots'.

Jenny skipped out of the lift and rushed to the outer doors urging her mum to hurry up.

Later in the morning, Gabe got a call from the second floor. Mrs Cole. Once again she was obviously not dressed for going out.

"Do you want a coffee, Gabe? I fancied a proper coffee and made myself a pot. Far too much for one, really."

"That would be lovely, Mrs Cole."

"Call me Ginny. How do you take it?"

"Lots of milk and two sugars, please."

"Won't be two ticks."

Soon she was back carrying a small tray with two cups and a plate of biscuits. Gabe took it off her and placed it on the table. He waited for Mrs Cole, Ginny, to be seated and passed both the cup and the plate. She helped herself to a couple of biscuits and sat back.

"Do you want to travel?" Gabe asked.

"No, let's just sit in the quiet." And so they did. The coffee was good and the biscuits crunchy and so only slurps and cracks were heard. Eventually, Ginny opened up the conversation. "You're a good man, Gabe."

Gabe blushed and looked surprised.

"How many other residents have come to you with their problems? Yet you never betray confidences. You never even hint at conversations passed. Thank you, Gabe."

Gabe looked genuinely nonplussed.

"I'm going to invite Phil for dinner sometime in the near future. I would like you to meet him. Get your seal of approval," she laughed.

"You don't need my 'seal of approval'. As long as he has yours."

"I know. But I would still like you to meet him. I'd like him to meet you, as well. I've told him about our lift chats. He's quite intrigued."

"I hope you haven't made me out to be anything special. I'll only fail on meeting."

She got up and placed her empty cup on the tray. Collected Gabe's and left, saying, "You won't Gabe."

Memoir of an Idiot

Robbie came to see me today. I thought he looked a bit upset and he confided in me that he was worried about going back to school; new teacher, harder work. I remembered that feeling. I didn't mind school. As I've said I was no brainbox but I did okay and most of the teachers were okay but it never stopped that first day back nerves. I think it was also to do with meeting back up with all those children. Most you hadn't seen over the holiday and you've become used to being one and then you're thrown back in and you're one of many. You have to re-establish your place in the mass. Yes. I could understand where Robbie was coming from.

I gave him a 'lucky feather'. I'm not sure I should have done. I just wanted him to have some self-confidence. He's a good kid. I'll have to come clean tomorrow. I hope his day goes well and that will help explain away the lie.

I wish all lies were that easily explained away. Terry had said he could take or leave the smack. It was about willpower and he never let onto Daz that he was a user. To be honest, he never looked like my image of a drug user, or a drug dealer come to that. But he was, and I was under the influence of his little bags.

Chapter 33

Robbie came flying into the lift, white feather grasped in his hand. "It worked, Gabe. I've had a good day and Mr Groves is okay. And guess what?" He rushed on before Gabe had time to answer, "I've been chosen for the school football team!"

"That's brilliant all ways round, Robbo."

"Do you need your feather back, now?" he said almost reluctantly.

"Actually, I've got a bit of a confession to make, Robbo. That's not a lucky feather. It's just a feather I found on the cushion."

Robbie stood open-mouthed.

"See Robbo. You went into school with a positive attitude because you thought you had something extra, but you didn't. It was just you. You made your own luck."

Robbie still looked bemused.

"You are your own luck. You don't need lucky feathers, or lucky anything else. Just be proud of who you are and what you can achieve."

"It wasn't lucky?"

Gabe shook his head.

"So how come I got into the football team?"

"You got in because you're good at football. What other reason could there be?"

Robbie was processing all this. Gabe could see the cogs turning. He was worried that Robbie would focus on the lie he'd told. He'd done it for the best, but did that justify it?

Robbie let the feather fall from his hand. "There's just one problem, though, Gabe. Football practice is on a Thursday evening after school. I don't think I can make The Lift Book Club as well."

"That's okay. We'll still be here, whenever you can make it."

Chapter 34

The first few weeks of term passed in the usual way. Robbie didn't make Thursdays, but the others met as usual. Sam had come along a couple of times and ended up talking to Miss James about a range of things. Who knew that such opposites would have so much in common?

One evening, just as Gabe was thinking about stopping for the night Mr Davies arrived home. Gabe had noticed that he'd been getting back later and later. He looked tense and made no eye contact. His hands twisted and turned on themselves. He became aware of this and viciously thrust them into his jacket pockets. He left the lift without a word and strode to his own flat door. Gabe hesitated by the lift doors. He was aware that Mr Davies stood there for a few seconds as though building up to something. He squared his shoulders and let himself in.

Gabe was reluctant to leave straight away. He remained on the second floor. He thought he heard a cry, cut off short. Muffled voices broke through the cracks in the door. Less than an hour after he entered Mr Davies reappeared with a large suitcase. He gave Gabe a suspicious stare, as he was waiting on the second floor, but made no comment.

The lift was silent except for the creaking and whirring of the mechanism. Mr Davies barely waited for the lift doors to open before he was charging through. He barged the outer doors and let them slam behind him.

*****

The car was still where John had left it less than an hour ago. He opened the rear door and swung his case onto the seat. He climbed into the passenger seat and sat rigidly. His hands were tight upon his knees and his shoulders seemed to want to touch his ears. A hand leant across and stroked his nearest hand. Under its gentle persistence, he relaxed and held the offered hand.

"I assume you told her?"

He nodded.

"How did she take it?"

He sat up straighter. "How do you think she took it? She's devastated. I've just blown her world up."

"Did you tell her about me?"

He nodded. "I don't think she was entirely surprised."

"Did you tell her about Birmingham?"

He nodded again. "I've told her everything. I've told her she will be financially secure and that I'd like access to Jenny, but we can sort that out later." His head dropped forward and he wiped his face with his hands. "She just looked at me. So shocked. So desperately trying to stay calm and not to wake Jenny. I didn't want to hurt her. I really didn't."

"I know. Perhaps when this first hurt is less you can have those kinds of conversations with her."

He shrugged tiredly. "I'm just wiped out. Living a lie for this last year, but now it's over I just feel empty."

"Come on. We'll go back to mine. Talk again in the morning. You're not working this week, are you?"

"No. Work said to take a week to start to get ready to move to Birmingham. They've got a place sorted for us there. At least as a stopgap."

"Let's go then."

Memoir of an Idiot

I think Mr Davies has left Jenny and Kathy. I could tell it wasn't easy for him, he looked like he could have cried when he came back out from the flat. I hope Kathy's all right. And little Jenny. How will she cope without her daddy at home? I was eight when my dad died. Did it have an impact on me? I'm sure it did but there was always Gran. It's not like Dad was a great one for kicking a ball about or taking me off to do 'men's' things.

I'll make sure I'm in early tomorrow and just check on them both before Jenny goes off to school. I'm sure Kathy will want her to go to school. Try and keep things as routine as possible. Life is more bearable if you have a routine.

That was my problem with Terry's little bags, no routine. I didn't even have the jobs for Daz anymore. Mrs G was chasing me from my room at nine and then the day just stretched ahead. Nowhere to go, nothing to do. I hung around kids' playgrounds or walked the streets staring into shop windows. Always my mind was on the itch crawling over my body, letting me know that I needed another bag.

Then I slipped even lower. I was in the shopping centre's loo when a guy put his phone on the edge of the washbasin whilst he washed his hand and walked towards the dryer. Without thinking I picked the phone up, hid it in my pocket and walked out. Once outside I legged it. Then I went and found Terry. He gave me three bags for the phone. I was in heaven.

Chapter 35

It was obvious the following morning that Mrs Davies and sleep and been indifferent friends in the night. Her face was pale, which only served to emphasise the dark circles under her eyes, the red rims of her eyes and the bright pink of her nose. No amount of cosmetic concealer was going to hide the devastation her face told of.

Neither was Jenny completely oblivious to the night's trauma. "My daddy is going to work away for a while," she said, seeking reassurance from the adults.

"Oh, daddy's have to do that sometimes. Good job your mummy's got you, isn't it?"

Jenny smiled. "Me and Mummy will have some fun times. Just her and me."

"Of course, you will. That will be great."

Mrs Davies smiled weakly. "Ok Chatterbox. Let's get you off to school."

She bravely pulled back her shoulders, took hold of Jenny's hand and stepped out of the lift.

Mrs Davies was soon back. She sat wearily in the armchair and picked mindlessly at the cracking leather. She looked up. "You saw him go." It was a statement.

Gabe gently nodded. "I'm sorry, Mrs Davies."

"Call me Kathy. I'm not Mrs. anything anymore." Silent tears seeped from her eyes. "He's been seeing someone else. For a year!"

Gabe had no reply. He sat and waited. "A year. I had no idea. It never crossed my mind. He said I must have guessed. But I hadn't. I honestly hadn't." She searched up her sleeve for her handkerchief. Dabbed at the tears now streaking her face. She choked on a sob. "Do you know what the worse thing is?"

She looked at Gabe as if expecting an answer. Gabe held his hands out in genuine confusion.

"He's left me for a man!" the last word came out on a wailing note. Gabe went and sat on the arm of the chair and clasped her to him. She leant her head into his chest and sobbed. Tears of anger. Tears of hurt.

Finally, she had sobbed herself dry. She pulled herself up straight and Gabe returned to the Captain's chair.

"Don't get me wrong. I don't have anything against gay people. But when my husband, when John says…" She trailed off.

Gabe leant forward, confidingly. "None of us can help who we love and from the look on John's face last night as he left, I would say he is also devastated. I think he loves you and Jenny. You are his family, but someone else now shares the space in his heart. He hasn't replaced you."

"Well, it damn well feels like it." There was a throb of anger in her voice.

"You know John far better than me, but do you think he would have waited a year to tell you if he wasn't afraid of hurting you?"

"But he has hurt me."

"And he knows that. But what should he have done? Carry on lying to you? Is that the sort of marriage you wanted? You're far too honest a person to want that, surely."

She sat looking at Gabe. Trying to make sense of what he had said and what she was feeling. She dropped her head onto one hand. "I don't know what to think. It's just going round and round in my head. One minute I think I have it straight and then another thought jumps up and knocks it all to pieces again."

"If I may make a suggestion?"

She looked at him.

"You need some sleep. You're not going into work today, are you?"

She shook her head, "I phoned in sick, a migraine. Which isn't that far from the truth."

"Go and have a hot bath. Put some gentle music on and go back to bed."

She shook her head again. "I'm worried that if I sleep too deeply I'll sleep through the alarm and not be there to pick Jenny up."

"Set your alarm, but I'll also promise to come and check that you are up an hour before you're due to go and collect Jenny. How's that?"

They had arrived on the second floor some time ago. Only now did Kathy push herself from the chair. Her movements were slow and heavy. "Thanks, Gabe," she said as she left.

Chapter 36

A little before Gabe was due to check on her he received a call from the second floor and it was Kathy. She had washed her hair and the darkness beneath her eyes was less pronounced. She saw the doors opening and just allowed a quick 'thumbs up' before she turned and walked away to her flat.

Later, when she left to collect Jenny, cosmetics had removed further signs of damage. Her tone was light and impersonal when she spoke to Gabe. "The weather is looking good."

Gabe agreed.

"We probably won't get many more days like these. I think I'll take Jenny to Swanton Park and maybe an ice cream."

Swanton Park was a large municipal park paid for by the factory owners back in the nineteenth century. It boasted a bandstand, a boating lake, complete with pedalos that looked like swans and walks through beautifully kept flower beds, no matter what the time of the year.

"That sounds lovely," Gabe said and genuinely meant it. "I envy you, especially the ice cream!"

She gave Gabe an artificially cheery wave as she left the lift. Gabe admired her strength and determination to carry on for Jenny's sake.

All further communication with Kathy retained this impersonal element. Jenny still attended The Lift Book Club, she didn't seem too perturbed by her father's absence, just once or twice mentioning that he was working away. Captain Clive still came two or three times a week and Mrs Cole dropped in from time to time. With the start of term, she had resumed her Conversational French classes, with Phil. Now with a more determined plan to have a holiday in France.

One evening, about two weeks since his departure Mr Davies arrived in the lift, just as Gabe was planning to finish for the night. He stood straight and tense, avoiding Gabe's eye.

"Evening, Mr Davies How are you?"

A flush of red ridged his cheeks. "Fine." He cleared his throat. "I, er." He coughed. "I understand from Kathy that you know something of our situation. And I, er, wanted to say 'Thank you'." His eyes met Gabe's at this last part.

Gabe put his palms up and shrugged. "I was just trying to help."

"Yes, I know. But Kathy said you helped her see things from my perspective."

"I just pointed out that there were other ways of looking at it."

The lift doors opened and Mr Davies approached Gabe, shook hands and left.

Gabe was quite sure that whatever happened tonight in the Davies household was not going to need his presence. The weekend after this meeting Mr Davies turned up to take Jenny out. She danced around him in the lift. Eager to be out and away. A little time after they'd left Kathy appeared in the lift. She made herself comfortable. Gabe thought she looked more relaxed. Not happy, but not angst-ridden.

"John said he saw you and thanked you. I need to thank you as well."

Gabe shook his head, "Really not necessary."

"We married very young, perhaps too young. Neither of us had had much experience with the opposite sex." She paused. Picking at the leather scratches. "John said," she waited and got herself under control. "John said, that he loves me. Loves us both, but never knew what it was like to fall head over heels in love." She emphasised the 'in love'.

Gabe waited.

"He said that at first, he was disgusted with himself. He had no experience of gay people. Looking back, he said, he had had crushes on boys when he was younger but put that down to hero-worship." She shifted in the chair and moved to the edge of the seat, elbows on her knees, leant forward. "Would you say I was mad if I told you that I felt sorry for him? Not angry, just terribly sorry."

"I think that shows remarkable compassion."

She leant back again. "Of course, I am still upset that I find myself a single mother, but if I'm honest, that's more about fear."

"That's only natural, but you are a remarkable woman for being so calm about it all. How's Jenny coping?"

"Better than I had hoped. It helps that John rings at bedtime and using one of these computer apps he can read her a bedtime story. And of course, coming to take her out today. I just hope she doesn't get upset again when he drops her back." She sighed deeply. "At the moment, we are telling her that Daddy has to work away. At some point, she is going to understand that he won't come back to live with us." She slapped her palms on her knees and rocked herself into a standing position. "But I'll deal with that when it happens."

Gabe opened the lift doors. Kathy took his hand and held it for a few seconds before walking out.

Chapter 37
Jenny Davies' Story

"Daddy doesn't live here anymore," said Jenny addressing Teddy, who sat up alert his button black eyes gazing attentively, "but that's okay because he'll still read us a bedtime story on his computer." She put Teddy to one side and picked up Becca, her ragdoll. "It will be different," she sighed and made a serious face, "I know you will miss the bedtime cuddle, but we can always cuddle each other." And she demonstrated a bear of a hug.

Jenny replaced Becca with Panda. A grubby mini stuffed toy with every sign of the sucking and chewing clear to see on his matted and bared skin. "I know you miss him, but he has to work away now. His work has sent him to Birmham." Her eyes misted. "Daddy still loves us. We are still his family."

She placed Panda with the other two. The three of them sat along the edge of her pillow, waiting for the next pearl of information. "Daddy's going to take me out on Saturday. That will be fun," she signed heavily again. "I know it won't be the same Panda, but we have to make the best of it."

She scooped up all three of them and held them close. "It will feel different for a little while, but soon it will be like it has always been this way." She rocked them from side to side. "And we can always have as many cuddles as we want, can't we." She took their muteness as consent and carried on squeezing and hugging.

Chapter 38

Robbie arrived late one evening to find The Lift Book Club remarkably full. The Captain. Sam and Mrs Cole were there as well as the regulars.

"Hi, Robbie. Thought we weren't going to see you today," said Gabe.

"Nah, had the dentist. No problems." He opened his mouth to show his teeth.

"Okay, let's have your reading book out."

"Gabe, can I ask you something first?" Without waiting for a reply he burrowed into his satchel and brought out his Rough book. "We got to do a project. All by ourselves. See." He thrust the book at Gabe.

Gabe flicked through it. "Hey, Robbo, you're writing's looking good." He kept turning the pages and came to a printed sheet stuck into the book. It read:

Year 5

Local History Project

Research something about the past in the area you live in. If you can, interview people about the past. Take photographs or do drawings to show some of your information.

Your project should be at least three pages of writing in your History book.

"I don't know what to do. What do you think?"

Gabe looked around the lift and said, "I think you have everything and everyone you need right in this lift, right this minute."

Robbie looked perplexed and then a light dawned and his face brightened. "Miss James and the ceramics factory!"

"Yes, and Mrs Cole, remember?"

"Oh, yeh. Oh, brill!"

Mrs Cole interrupted. "You can use some of the information in my book but you must use your own words; otherwise, it's plagiarism." Seeing Robbie's unfamiliarity with the word, she elaborated, "Cheating."

"Right, yeh," he nodded vigorously. "So, I think the first thing you need to do, Robbie, is write down a plan of action," she continued.

Robbie rummaged for his pencil and started a fresh page in his Rough book. Pencil poised he looked up for guidance.

"Okay," said Mrs Cole going into teacher mode. "First decision: are you going to research all the old ceramic factories in Swanton or just Etherington's?"

Robbie thought. "Just Etherington's. Don't you think?"

She agreed. "Now what research do you need to do?"

Robbie looked blank.

"Well, you need to find out when Etherington's started and finished."

"Don't forget the Etherington name is still going," interjected Miss James.

"So as well as interviewing Miss James you could see if someone still working at the factory would see you."

"I could help there," added Miss James.

In under an hour, Robbie had his plan mapped out. He was going to take Mrs Cole's book into school because he could work on it during his History session. He was going to ask his mum if Mrs Cole could take him to the library for more research. He would interview Miss James next week, and in the meantime, she was going to contact the factory and see if they could visit. Captain Clive had offered to escort them and loan Robbie his digital camera. "Don't know how it works. When ready I take it to the photo shop in town. Nice chap. Good photos."

Chapter 39

Robbie's project seemed to put a bit of vibrancy into everyone. Although Robbie did take Mrs Cole's book into school it also became his Lift Book Club reader as well. He read sections and then he, with Gabe's help, worked out which bits he needed.

Robbie read, "Etherington's Ceramics was founded in 1796 by George Etherington." He paused and then said, "Well, I could just write that, eh?"

"You could, but it wouldn't be your own words, would it?"

"No, but how else can I say it?"

"What does 'founded' mean?"

"I thought it meant started."

"Okay, so wouldn't you say 'started' rather than 'founded'?"

"I see, yeh."

"And you could write the information in a different order."

Robbie gazed at the sentence for a while and then said, "So I could write 'George Etherington started his ceramic factory in 1796'?"

Mrs Cole clapped, "Well done, Robbie. You've used the information but used your own words."

Another time everyone chipped in with ideas about what questions he should ask Miss James, whilst she busied herself with hearing Jenny read. One question he didn't save for the interview had everyone interested, "Miss James, do you know how they make the cups and things in the factory?"

"Oh, yes. I don't think the process will have changed much since I was in the factory. Mr Etherington insisted that I know every stage of the process so that I understood any queries or problems on the shop floor."

"What shop?"

"That's what you call the area where the work is done, the shop floor."

Robbie wrote this down. "So how do they make it?"

*****

"Right, Miss James, I'm going to leave you with Harry, here, who will show you the factory and how we operate."

Harry tipped his cloth cap and said, "Right you are Mr Etherington. Miss James," and he indicated that she should proceed him down the spiral metal staircase. Their footsteps clanged out of synch and were quite cacophonous by the time they reached the bottom.

"Right we'll start in the casting section. Hang on a minute." He disappeared into the staffroom beneath the offices. On his return, he had a brown overall coat. "You better put this on, Miss. They do splash about in the casting room."

At first, Miss James thought she was watching cooks at work. Four men, in clay splattered dungarees and collarless undershirts, were ladling a white/grey slop, from a large bowl clasped to their chest by their left arm, into containers on bars laid across what looked like enormous earthenware sinks. "That there is the slip," Harry explained.

"What's slip?"

"Slip is liquid clay, and they're ladling into moulds. Those are cups and their handles."

"Oh, I thought you would have potter's wheels."

Harry laughed. "No, Miss. Not feasible. We wouldn't be able to produce enough sets if we did it that way."

Miss James watched as each man came to the end of his row and put the ladle and bowl down. They then returned to the beginning of their section and began to turn the mould over, emptying out the slip.

Then each man loaded his moulds onto a plank and, it seemed, effortlessly lifted it onto his shoulder and walked over to great empty racks, waiting for their shelves of moulds. Miss James noticed that further away, along the array of racks, someone else was taking off the planks of moulds and carrying them to a different section.

Harry tapped her arm and led her after this last man. In another section of the factory, men were opening the moulds and releasing their contents. "That's called cracking, Miss. Opening up the moulds. If you do it too early the clay won't have set and leave it too long and the clay is harder to release."

As each item was released it was inspected and sat on another plank. Miss James noticed that when it came to the handles the men had small knives in their hands. Harry noticed her gaze. "That's trimming. Don't often need to do it for the bigger items, but fiddly things like handles, you have to make sure they're nice and clean, ready to be put onto the cups."

They continued the tour. In another section, she saw the handles being attached to teapots, using more of the slip, she guessed. The next section was partitioned off and there were women seated at desks, busy rubbing and sponging the cups and their handles. "They're fettling, Miss. See, you get a seam when you mould cast so these girls are rubbing away the seam print."

"Why is it all women? Why was it all men in the previous parts?"

"Well. Most of the work, up to this point is messy, and some of it heavy work. Here we need a lighter touch. Fettle too much and the clay becomes too thin and could crack in the firing."

Each woman was filling a crate with cups ready for the next stage. Harry beckoned her to follow him again. At the end of the room, two women were dipping the clay objects into a clear liquid and draining them on a wheeled trolley, about six feet wide and tall. "This a sealing glaze ready for the first firing."

As they walked further on Miss James became aware of the heat building. The factory was always warm, but this was furnace hot. "These are our firing kilns." Shouted Harry above the roar emanating from each kiln. Further on the kilns were quieter, just the sound of fans. "We're cooling them down ready to open," Harry explained.

The clay will be glazed and fired a second time before we decorate them." He then took her into a separate room, where again, more women were seated, but the air was hushed. "This is where we put on transfers and any paintwork we want. Again women have the more delicate touch. And here we have Jose and Mary, our guilders."

Miss James watched as each woman loaded a fine paintbrush with gold paint and painted a perfect rim on a rotating plate. It was quite breath-taking. Time and time again, a perfect rim. "What sort of paint is that?"

"That," said Harry proudly, "Is twenty-two-carat liquid gold!"

"But doesn't it scratch off?"

"It'll have another, its fourth firing when Jose and Mary have finished. That stops some of the wearing. The final part of the process is to wrap up the stock ready for dispatch." He led her into the final section of the factory. Workbenches were laid out, each laid with parts of a tea or dinner service. An elderly man was *working at one of them. He was inspecting each item before wrapping it in tissue paper and, Miss James leaned over to look, placing them in a packing chest.*

"Right, Miss. Now you've seen everything here. You know about the invoices and bills of fare, don't you?"

"Yes. Thank you, Harry. I hadn't realised what a long and intricate process it was and how much skill goes into making it all. It really was beautiful to watch."

Harry smiled as he took the overall from her. "Beautiful indeed, Miss."

Memoir of an Idiot

Robbie's project seems to have breathed new life into everyone. Tomorrow Miss James and the Captain are taking Robbie to see what remains of the Etherington factory. Miss James still has a contact there who is willing to show Robbie around. They are all so excited. I feel chuffed on their behalf.

I thought the stealing of the mobile was the lowest of the low. I didn't dare go back to the centre in case they'd ID'd me from CCTV. Every time I walked down the street I was on the lookout for the bloke in case he'd found out who'd stolen it and was after me. But that was nothing compared to the insatiable need for Terry's little bags.

Then Terry suggested I try a different dealer, "His stuff ain't as good as Daz's. I don't know what he cuts it with but it is cheaper." That should have told me enough. Daz was known as a safe dealer because of what he used to cut it with. This was a whole different ball game.

One night Mrs G tried to talk to me. She said she was worried about how thin I'd got and had I spoken with my mum. I tried to reassure her. Said I was fine. "But you're not working, are you?" Every syllable was an accusation. I told her it was just a blip. I was out looking. Not to worry and escaped to my room. I don't think she believed me. I was wondering whether she would phone Mum, but nothing came that night.

The next day I knew my social had come through so I went to find this new dealer, Smike, with cash in my pocket. He was a bit cagy to start with until I explained that Terry had sent me. I bought five bags while I had the cash. Never mind it wouldn't leave very much for food. Who needs food when you can sail somewhere else with your little bag?

Chapter 40

Miss James had been able to organise that she, the Captain and Robbie could visit the remaining part of Etherington's ceramics. Robbie, with Mrs Cole's help, had created a diagram showing the various stages of the ceramics process as explained by Miss James. His mum had been able to laminate it at work as he wanted to take it with him on the visit to see if anything had changed since Miss James' time.

Captain Clive had given Robbie instructions about how to use the camera. Gabe smiled to himself because it was obvious that Robbie knew exactly what to do, but was polite enough to allow the Captain to do his bit.

The day of the visit was a wet one and Gabe had organised for a taxi to take the three of them to the factory. Miss James had relinquished her three-wheeled walker for a four-pronged walking stick and the use of the Captain's arm. There was an air of a holiday outing amongst the three of them. Gabe waved them off.

On their return, they were full of news. Robbie had seen the processes. Apparently, not much had changed in the actual process, just some of the equipment was newer and easier to use. Captain Clive had been thoroughly entertained by it all and Robbie had taken "Hundreds of photos." He'd also been given two tea plates: one before all the firing and decorating processes and the other a finished item. "I'm going to make them part of my project. Do you think that'll be okay?"

"I think that would be wonderful," Gabe said.

"Miss James was also quite happy. The foreman on the shop floor had been a 'gofer' when she was last at the factory."

"What's a gofer?"

"Someone who is at the bottom of the pile and people are always telling them to 'go for this' and 'go for that'. So they're called 'go fors or gofer," Miss James explained.

This young man, Clyde, had worked himself up through the ranks, just as his father before him had. Apparently, the whole family had put their redundancy money into buying the equipment from old Mr Etherington, who true to his word had given them their current workplace, free of charge and allowed them to continue using the name.

"It's a going concern now, but there's only sixteen of them. They just do special commissions and celebration pieces. They're planning a commemoration mug for the next VE Day celebrations."

"What with all the stuff Miss James has given me and going to the factory I've got tons for my project. I'm going to ask Sir if I can do it on paper, not in my book, so I can use all my photos and diagram."

Robbie rode with them all to the third floor and saw both Captain Clive and Miss James' to their doors. Gabe listened as he said his thank yous and could hear the genuineness in his voice. On the way back down, Gabe said, "Do you remember in the front of Mrs Cole's book she had what's called a dedication page? The bit where she said Thank you to her husband and a friend?"

"Yeh." But Robbie was ahead of him, "I could do that for Miss James, the Captain and Mrs Cole, couldn't I?"

"You could, and I think they would be very proud."

Chapter 41

One Thursday evening Robbie unexpectedly turned up. "Hi, Robbo. No football practise tonight?"

"Nah." Robbie slumped on the stool next to Miss James, as Jenny wasn't with them this evening. "Mr Groves has broken his ankle."

"Oh, wow! That's bad luck for him. Is he okay, apart from his ankle?"

"Yeh. He fell over on the ice at playtime yesterday and had to go to the hospital. He came into school today but he has to have it resting on a chair and can't walk around very good. We've got to be extra well behaved, Mrs Fisher said so."

"I'm sorry to hear that. So no football practice or matches for the rest of this term, then?"

"Mr Groves said, for the rest of the season, unless somebody's dad or big brother, or even mum, he said, could take the practices. I don't think they will, and we was third in the league. We could have made the top, we're only two points behind." Robbie's head sunk even lower. There was silence in the lift. Only Miss James and Sam were in today. Robbie sighed deeply again and then asked, "What about you, Gabe? You could take the practice for us. Couldn't you?"

"Sorry, mate, but I don't know much about football."

"Mr Groves said he would still come to practice, he just can't do all the training and stuff."

"I can't leave the lift, Robbie. I'd lose my job."

"Oh, yeh," Robbie sighed again.

"Come on then. Are you reading tonight?"

"Nah. I'm still working on my project. Mr Groves said I can do it on paper and Mum has given me a hard file to keep it in. See you later."

"Okay. See you tomorrow."

Robbie left, and the lift company went back to reading their own books. Gabe had noticed Sam look up when Robbie was talking about needing someone to take football practice. "Do you play football, Sam?"

Sam looked up and laid his book face down on his lap. "I used to. Like Robbie, I was in the school team, right up until I left, in fact."

"You must have been good, then."

"I was fast. They played me in wing and I could outrun most other players," he said modestly.

"Ever taken a team practice?"

Sam smiled, "I know where this is going, Gabe. With my shift work, I'd have to miss some."

"True, but the boys missing one or two practices across the weeks is better than missing them all."

"And the same goes for weekends. You know I'm often working the weekends."

"Yeh. But Robbie didn't mention weekends. They just need someone for the Thursday evenings."

Sam sighed and made a show of turning his book back over to read.

"Just a thought," was Gabe's final comment.

Chapter 42

Ice and falls seemed to be a theme. A couple of days later Miss James decided she needed a walk. "I'm getting moth-eaten, indoors all the time." The day was bright, with little wind, but there had been a hard frost the night before.

"You take care, Miss James. Are you going up to the cemetery?"

"Yes. I won't be long." With a jaunty wave, she thanked Gabe for managing the outer doors for her and set off.

With the cold air, Gabe expected her back within the hour. She didn't arrive. Nearing two hours he was beginning to be seriously worried and was considering abandoning the lift and setting out to find her. Just as he had resolved to do this a skinny young man, padded out with a parka, balaclava and hat, stood at the lift doors. "Excuse me mate, are you Gabe?"

Gabe stood up, "Yes. Is it Miss James?"

"The old dear with this three-wheeled walker?" he pointed to Miss James' wheeler beside him.

"Yes."

"Yeh. She's had a fall." As Gabe went to dash out of the lift he grabbed his arm. "Hang on mate. She's okay. I called an ambulance and wrapped her in my stock cloth to keep warm. They've taken her to A&E and she asked me to tell you what happened."

"Right," Gabe breathed out deeply.

"The paramedic reckoned she was lucky and hadn't broken anything, but they'll do an x-ray to check. She said she hoped to be home this evening but probably wouldn't come to the book club?"

Gabe smiled. "Right. Yes. She's a regular member. I'll let the others know. Thanks for coming to tell me. I was getting worried."

"She's a game old bird. Even after she'd fallen she kept chatting. Something about she'd been telling her friend all about a young man who's doing a project on where they used to work. I'm never sure with her how much is real!"

"Yeh, I know. But she's much more with it; then she'd have you believe."

"Okay then. See yer!" With that, he traipsed across the foyer leaving little specks of soil behind.

Gabe marvelled at the kindness of strangers.

He waited until late afternoon and then travelled to the third floor and Sam's flat. He knocked quietly on the door, not wanting to wake him if he hadn't got up yet. He only had to wait a few seconds and the door opened.

"Gabe. Is there a problem?"

Gabe explained about Miss James and her fall. "I just wondered if you could look in and find out how she is. How bad it is. I don't imagine she'll be home tonight."

"Of course. I hope she hasn't broken anything. It's often the first stage in their decline with people of her age. Let me have your mobile number and I'll ring you."

"Ah. I don't have a mobile." Gabe thought for a moment. "Check with me on your way to work and I'll have one of the residents' number's for you."

When Gabe heard Robbie and Alison come in he stepped out of the lift.

"Hi, Gabe," Robbie smiled.

"Hi ya, Robbie. Alison, could I have a word, please?"

Once again she looked wary, so Gabe rushed to explain about Miss James and Sam's checking on her "It's just that I don't have a mobile and I wondered if I could ask you to take the message from Sam, just so we know what's happening."

"Oh, no. Poor Miss James. Yes, of course. Let me get into the flat and I'll write it down for you to give to Sam."

"Is she really hurt?" Robbie asked concernedly.

"The chap, I think he must be a gardener at the cemetery, said the paramedic didn't think she'd broken anything, but they have to check."

Robbie nodded and followed his mum into their flat.

An hour later Robbie appeared with an envelope and a piece of paper. "The paper's got our phone number on it for Sam and the card is for Miss James." He placed both carefully in Gabe's hand.

Chapter 43

Miss James arrived home in style by ambulance and wheelchair. One foot was stretched out imperiously in front, bound professionally in tight, white bandages. The ambulance staff wheeled her in and said to Gabe. "We understand that the hospital has spoken with a Ms White, who is going to look after Miss James, is she here?"

Gabe had seen Alison go out, but not return, but at that moment Alison stepped out of her flat. "Hello there. Yes, I'm here." She then addressed Miss James, "Morning, Miss James. You understand that you're going to spend a couple of nights with me?"

"Yes, dear. But I really don't want to be a bother."

"It's no bother, I promise and it's only until you can put weight properly on your ankle and then we'll move you back to your flat?"

"Yes, my dear. This is very kind of you. But I couldn't stand spending any more time in the hospital. I don't know how people sleep in there. I've not had a wink."

"Oh, there not meant for sleeping, my love," said the elder of the two ambulance staff. "Now you're home you can have a nap."

"But what about your work, Alison? You can't be having time off."

"It's not a problem. I explained that Robbie's grandmother had had a fall and they've given me two days compassionate leave. Then it's the weekend. So we don't have to worry until Monday."

Miss James' eyes filled up.

"In you come then. Do you want to sit up or have a nap?"

"I'd love a proper cup of tea and then, yes, I think I will have a sleep," Gabe heard Miss James reply as she was wheeled in through Alison's front door.

Later, Robbie explained that Miss James was in his bedroom and she had been admiring his project. "It's got to be handed in on Monday, but it's just about finished. I haven't put that stuff in about Miss James, the Captain and Mrs Cole yet. But I will. Mum thought it was a lovely idea."

Miss James was too tired to attend The Lift Book Club that night. But Robbie wheeled her through the following night and she took up her usual duties.

"Guess what," Robbie said, once Miss James was settled and the brakes firmly pulled.

"What about?"

"Someone's going to do our football practice. Mr Groves said that someone had contacted him and they could start next week. Yippee! We've got a really big match in two weeks against Trosnant. They're top of the league, but Mr Groves said he thinks we can beat them."

"That's great news. So we won't be seeing you on Thursdays again?"

"Sorry, Gabe."

"Not a problem. We're always here. Whenever you're ready."

By the Sunday evening, Miss James was ready to go back to her own flat. Her ankle was still obviously painful to walk on but she could manage with the aid of her wheeled walker. However, she had agreed that she would still eat with Alison and Robbie as she didn't trust herself with hot pans and a poorly foot. As Robbie helped her in for her home-ward journey she said, "Such a lovely young woman. So kind. I don't know what I would have done without her kindness. And this young man," she patted Robbie's arm, "has been so caring and considerate. I feel really well looked after."

Robbie blushed but looked pleased.

Each evening Miss James made the journey down to the ground floor for her supper before attending the book club. Mrs Cole, when she learnt of Miss James' accident, had offered to do any shopping she needed and checked in on her at lunchtime to make sure she'd had something to eat.

"What a wonderful little community we have," said Miss James.

The Captain also became a regular visitor to Miss James' flat as they discovered that they both had a passion for chess. From the discussions that continued at the book club, Gabe got the impression that they were evenly matched. It soon transpired that the Captain was visiting in the morning as well and he became responsible for their lunches.

"I don't mind," said Mrs Cole, smiling. "They so obviously enjoy their matches and I would only get in their way."

Chapter 44

Two things of importance happened on Friday of the following week. Robbie rushed in clasping a lever arch file. "Gabe, Gabe. Guess what."

Gabe smiled and shrugged.

"Look." Robbie thrust the file at him. Gabe opened and read. It was Robbie's Etherington project, complete with diagrams and photos. The dedication page was at the front and read:

"Thank you to Miss James, Captain Clive, Mrs Cole and my mum for helping me."

"That's really nice," said Gabe.

"Yeh, but read to the end," Robbie urged.

As Gabe turned the final page he could see what Robbie was so pleased about. There were levels and numbers but most prominent was not one, but two gold stars and clearly written the comment:

"Robbie. This is a wonderful project. Probably the best Year 5 project I have ever marked. I liked your diagram explaining how cups and plates are made and well done for going to visit the factory. 10/10 for effort."

"Wow, Robbo. That is amazing. Have you shown Miss James and the others yet?"

"No. I thought I'd show it to you first and then them."

Miss James and the Captain arrived together and the Captain leant over Miss James' shoulder to read the project with her. They were both deeply touched by the dedication and delighted at the result.

Somewhat gruffly the Captain said, "Well done, young man. Fine project."

Miss James wanted to give Robbie a hug, which he bravely endured.

Gabe knew that Mrs Cole was out but said to Robbie that he would let her know that he wanted to show his project to her. At this point Sam joined them, dragging the inevitable bean bag.

"And that's the other thing," shouted Robbie, dancing with excitement again. "Sam is taking our football practice!"

Sam looked a little sheepish. "I thought about what you said, Gabe. It seemed mean not to help out if I could."

"He's really good," said Robbie admiringly. "Mr Groves said that now there's no excuse for not winning the league with such a good coach."

Sam held up his hands. "Whoa, there Robbie. I'm just one man. It's the team, all eleven of you that are going to win the league. I can just help out. But in the end, it's down to you and your teammates."

"Yeh. I know." Turning to Gabe again, "But he's really good."

Everyone laughed and Sam quickly sat down and hid in his book.

Chapter 45

The day of the Trosnant match dawned clear and bright. By chance, Sam was on his last night shift and so forwent his sleep to go along and support the team. It was a home match so Alison was also going and so the three of them all set off together. Alison and Sam had not met many times, but Robbie was the perfect foil for any discomfort they may have felt in one another's presence. Later that morning Miss James and Captain Clive appeared together, waiting at the lift doors. Miss James' ankle was still weak and so she wore a discreet bandage, barely visible above her short ankle boots. Both were dressed for the cold. Miss James in her usual beret, scarf and coat; black gloves waiting to be put on. The Captain wore a long, black wool coat. So often preferred by those who marched past the cenotaph each year. He also wore a black scarf and gloves and held a trilby in his hand.

"Lovely day for a walk. Are you going anywhere special?" Gabe asked as they seated themselves.

"We're going to the cemetery," answered Miss James. "I haven't visited since my fall."

"So going to be her wingman," said the Captain smiling broadly. "Can't be having any more falls."

No, and I did want to see if that nice young man was there as well. He was so kind to me and I don't think I really thanked him properly."

"I think you probably did," said Gabe. "He was full of admiration for you."

Miss James tutted. "Silly old woman not looking where I was going." She pulled on her gloves with some determination.

"It could happen to anyone. Look at what Robbie's teacher did. I think you were very lucky."

"Yes, you're right. And everyone has been so kind to me since. Even this dear man," she smiled, indicating the Captain.

"Needed a chess partner. Not many women can play as well as she can." His face was partially covered as he moved to put his hat on.

Gabe ignored the non-pc view behind this and, instead, admired the sentiment in the praise intended.

Gabe watched as the Captain gallantly held the outer doors to enable Miss James to manoeuvre through. As they were making their way down the path he saw a man stop and make an enquiry of them. Gabe judged that he was asking for Harrington Hall as both Miss James and the Captain pointed back the way they had just come.

The man was of average height and a little stout, but perhaps that was only because he was wrapped in a chunky duffle coat. He had a fine face, Gabe thought. Open and pleasant. Greying hair and lines around his eyes and across his forehead gave him a mature bearing but not old.

Gabe waited by the lift as the man came through the doors, taking off his gloves as he came in from the cold. As he approached the lift he called out, "Hello, are you Gabe?"

Gabe knew at one this was Mrs Cole's. Phil. "Yes, and you must be Phil. Sorry, Mrs Cole never told me your last name."

"That's okay. Phil's fine. Ginny has told me a lot about..." His voice trailed off as he stepped into the lift. "Oh, my goodness. She wasn't lying about the nomadic room." He espied Robbie's poster, "Or the Lift Book Club." He shook his head in wonder. "This is really lovely. What a wonderful idea."

Gabe pressed for the second floor as Phil looked at the bookshelf and studied the rules. "Ah, so I couldn't be a member?"

"'Fraid not. I'm only allowed because I work here."

The doors opened and Gabe pointed wordlessly to Mrs Cole's door.

"Thanks. Won't be long. I'm taking Ginny out for lunch."

With that in mind, Gabe waited on the second floor. Only minutes later Mrs Cole and Phil appeared at the lift doors. "Morning Gabe. You've met Phil?"

"Yes."

"Of course, you have! Sorry, silly question." Mrs Cole was a little flustered. Whether it was having Phil here on her own territory or because of meeting Gabe was unclear.

"Phil says you're going out for lunch."

"Yes, we're going to try the College Kitchen. Do you know about it?"

Gabe shook his head.

"It's the catering students at the college. Two days a week they run like a restaurant cooking set menus for anyone who wants to book. But on a Saturday they experiment with flavours and methods of cooking. Apparently, it's literally pot luck what you get. But we're game, aren't we?" She addressed this last sentence to Phil.

"As long as spicy things are spicy, but not hot, I'll be fine. But I did bring my antacids with me." He winked at Gabe as a co-conspirator.

Gabe smiled and Mrs Cole tapped Phil on the arm. "Don't. I'm sure it will be lovely."

Gabe watched this couple through the outer doors and down the path. He watched as Mrs Cole put her arm through Phil's as they set off towards the town centre.

That just left Mrs Davies and Jenny. Gabe wondered what they were up to today. The answer, for at least part of that question, arrived at the lift, Mr Davies. "Morning Gabe. How are you?"

Mr Davies was much more upbeat than he had been on previous visits. "Jenny is coming to Birmingham for the whole weekend." He grinned infectiously and rapidly strode to his former home, knocking sharply on the door.

Once again Gabe stayed on the second floor. Several minutes later Jenny appeared with her little school rucksack on her back and her daddy with a small suitcase, more like the old fashioned vanity cases women had. Mrs Davies appeared at the door. Jenny turned back to give her a huge hug and then skipped towards the lift. Mr Davies said a few words and followed her.

"Gabe, I'm going to see and stay at daddy's new house and I'm going to have my very own room there as well."

"Wow! That's fantastic. You've got all the stuff you need," Gabe pointed at the rucksack.

"Most of it, and daddy has some things in that case." Pointing to the one Mr Davies held aloft.

As usual, when not occupied, Jenny made a beeline for the leather armchair. Gabe noted that her feet now overlapped the edge of the seat. It seemed like only a few weeks ago that they were several inches short of the end.

Jenny skipped out of the lift, shouting "Bye, Gabe. Daddy, come on."

Mr Davies smiled and hurried after her.

Gabe worried about Kathy Davies. Her first time without Jenny. But he needn't have. An hour or so after Jenny had left Kathy called for the lift. She too carried a small suitcase.

"Off anywhere nice?" Gabe said eyeing the case.

"A friend of mine; she knows about John leaving and having Jenny this weekend, so she's invited me over. We're having a night out this evening and lunch out tomorrow."

"That's a brilliant idea. I'm so pleased."

"Yes. Me too. Just spending this last hour without Jenny around was quite bad enough. It's silly because I'm often in the flat alone when Jenny's at school, but this just felt different."

"I'm sure it does. It will become more familiar. You may even get to the point when a weekend off from teenage tantrums is a blessed relief," Gabe jibed.

Kathy smiled. "I expect you're right about that. And she is growing up so fast."

Kathy left the lift. She waved Gabe goodbye as she left the building.

Chapter 46

All those that returned to Harrington Hall that afternoon did so with good cheer. First were the Captain and Miss James. Gabe espied them as they turned up the path to Harrington Hall's entrance. They were deep in conversation and very animated. As they entered the lift Gabe heard Captain Clive say, "I'll cook us a spot of lunch, Ilene. You go and freshen up and I'll make a start."

"Oh, Roger, that would be lovely. Perhaps we could finish that chess game from yesterday?"

"Ah, Gabe. Good morning's walk."

"Did you find the young man who helped you?"

"I did and I thanked him," Miss James beamed. "He was so nice. He works for the Parks Department and is based in the cemetery. He likes to keep it looking nice."

"Yes. Good chap. Doesn't want it looking scruffy if family drop in. Not a lot of young people think like that these days," added the Captain.

Miss James sat in the armchair and the Captain stood close at hand.

"How was your ankle?" Gabe asked solicitously.

"Absolutely fine. I could probably take the bandage off, but it just reassures me."

Gabe left them on the third floor still planning the rest of the day.

Next came Robbie. Gabe heard him before he saw him, "We are the champions!" he flew across the foyer and into the lift. "We won, Gabe. We thrashed them Four–one! You should have seen their faces. We're top of the league on goal difference." He skipped about. In and out of the lift until Alison and Sam appeared. They were both laughing at Robbie's antics.

"Careful, Robbie," Alison warned.

"Don't be getting too cocky, we're only top of the league, this week. We've still got plenty of matches left to play," Sam warned.

"Yeh, but they were the strongest team and we beat them!"

"Well, even if you're now seen as the strongest team, doesn't mean another team can't beat you, does it?" Sam pointed out.

Robbie looked thoughtful, but then broke into "We are the Champions…this week!"

The three adults laughed.

"Right, Robbie. We need to get you home and into the bath. Look at your knees," Alison said and then turned to Sam. "You're welcome to come in for a cuppa while I get him clean."

"That's really kind, but I really do need to get to bed."

Alison looked a little downcast, Gabe thought.

"Can I take rain check?" Sam continued. "I'll probably sleep the clock round, but would love to pop in for a cuppa tomorrow, late afternoon?"

"Yes. I'd like that."

"But I'm going to the Film Club," Robbie pouted.

"That's okay," Alison said, "Sam could come after that. About five?"

"Love to. Now I must get to bed." To emphasise the point he gave a jaw cracking yawn.

"Come on then," Gabe said and pressed the third-floor button. Robbie and Alison stood and waved as the doors closed.

"She's a nice lady," Sam said.

"I've always thought so," replied Gabe.

Sam nodded slowly as the lift ascended. As he walked out Gabe called, "Sleep tight!"

The final returnee was Mrs Cole, Ginny. She was on her own but walked lightly and smiled broadly when Gabe welcomed her into the lift.

"Lovely day, Gabe. Phil and I had a lovely lunch and then went to the Exhibition in the museum. You know the one about Treasure Hoards?"

Gabe shook his head.

"Oh, you must go. I might suggest to Mrs White that I take Robbie. I think he'd be fascinated. There are swords and axes, helmets and shields and lots and lots of jars full of coins. What do you think?"

"Robbie would love it. He seems to be into history, but he'll definitely want to look at the weapons."

"Yes. That's what I thought. I'll drop down and talk to her later."

Later that afternoon she did go and see Alison and Robbie about the trip. Robbie was delighted and all was arranged for the following morning.

Memoir of an Idiot

It's been a fantastic weekend. Every resident was out doing something that added colour and value to their lives. I think Sam and Alison are going to get on and Robbie acts as a natural interest for both of them. The Captain and Miss James seem to have found a comfortable routine with each other. Kathy Davies is creating a life beyond being a mum and Ginny Cole is happy with her chap, Phil.

My Gran used to say something like, "It does you good to see it." 'It's being whatever she was seeing or watching, but I think I understand what she means now. I felt good seeing my residents feeling good. Daft I know. But there you are. It's amazing how involved I feel with all of them. Now I wonder why I had to find this kind of contentment in little bags.

For a few weeks, I was okay for money and Smike was always to be found but then, inevitably, I ran out of funds and Smike wasn't the type to let you have anything on tick. Mind you neither would Terry. I had seriously asked around to see if anywhere wanted casual labour. I got a few hours with the Indian shopkeeper. He's just had a large order and needed to revamp his storeroom. For a few hours, I was lugging pallets across the floor. Some were half empty and shifted easy, but others were really loaded. I thought I was going to pop a blood vessel with one of them. That got me £40. I was sensible at that moment, I was tired, thirsty and hungry so I did go and have an all-day breakfast with unlimited mugs of tea at the local cafe. But my next call was on Smike.

I decided to go back to the café. I had this idea in my mind that I might be able to do a phone swipe again. I'd noticed when I was in there before that people often played on their phones until their food arrived and then just left it on the table. Even walking away to the toilets and leaving it there. I might get a chance.

I made a cup of coffee last half a morning and I did think at one point that I was going to have a go but the guy was only going to get another napkin rather than go to the loo. Not getting very far I made to leave. The café owner asked me if I was looking for work. I wondered if he'd guessed why I was there. He went on to explain that his normal counter girl was off sick and he needed someone to do the pots. Could I operate an industrial dish washer? I said I'd never tried but would give it a go for cash in hand.

It was dead simple. I stacked up trays, slid them into the machine and closed it. It did the work and I emptied clean crockery. Dirk was his name. He was going to explain about being named after Dirk Bogarde and who he was but I told him about me and Gran watching the older films. He offered the same gig and rate for the rest of the week. I jumped at the chance.

I used the little bags to just keep me revved and I worked well. On Thursday, Dirk's deep fat fryer went sick and the engineer couldn't make it until Monday. Dirk was in a right panic. No chips with the Friday and Saturday night crowds coming up. I offered to have a look at it, and with a little persuading, he allowed me to. I knew straight away that it was the thermostat. Dirk phoned around and found a place that sold them but he couldn't leave the shop and asked me to go.

I didn't mind going, what I minded was the £100 burning in my pocket. Dirk doesn't do cards, cash only. I felt pleased that he'd given me the money without batting an eye but the temptation to take it to find Smike was unbearable. I sat on the 22 bus and tried to think of something else. Anything else. I thought about Bogarde films Gran and I had watched. Then about how many Carry-On films I could list. Anything but the money in my pocket. I have never been so pleased to hand over £100 than I was when I bought the thermostat.

Chapter 47

Autumn was rapidly moving into winter and yet Gabe felt that Harrington Hall had never felt more alive. Sam continued with the coaching for Robbie's school team and managed to get to most of their games. And, despite his warning, Robbie's team were still top of the league. Alison would go to the matches if they were home games and frequently Sam would go in for a cuppa on their return to the flats, but that was as far as it went. Sam's shift and Alison's commitments to work and Robbie gave neither of them much spare time.

Robbie still attended The Lift Book Club and continued to work his way through the Harry Potter series. Miss James and Jenny were avid listeners. Kathy Davies was a more frequent attendee now, but she also seemed to have a spring in her step. John had Jenny every other weekend and Kathy had increased her hours at the chemist so that she worked every other Saturday. She'd also discovered that she liked the social side of working with, mainly, women and it wasn't unusual for her to be out on a Saturday evening if Jenny was away. "Making up for lost time," she half-jokingly said to Gabe one evening when she was off to another 'girls' night out'.

Ginny Cole was still happy with Phil and the French Conversation class. Phil was a regular visitor to Harrington Hall; sometimes to take Ginny out, but sometimes for an evening in. Gabe had got to know him through these visits and felt that he was a genuine man and that he was good for Ginny. She had never been a 'stay at home' type and Gabe knew that she had had an active social life before Phil's appearance. In fact, she told Gabe that she made a point of staying in touch with her friends, "Having a man around is very nice, but old friends are a treasure you must never waste."

But the best of all, as far as Gabe was concerned, was the growing friendship between Miss James and Captain Clive. They were regular travellers in the lift these days. Captain Clive acted as Miss James' 'wingman', and they went out regardless of winds! Their days were spent in one another's flats and endless games of chess or gourmet meals were planned. One night, the Captain even took her to the Ladies' Night at The Old Comrades. "I shall have to keep an eye on her," said the Captain as they rode down in the lift, "Those chaps see an attractive woman they'll knock me aside." Miss James laughed and patted his arm. "I'm quite happy with this fine chap."

Gabe wondered if Michael might think he had done his community service. The residents of Harrington Hall now knew and communicated with one another and, as Miss James had said, they now had a fine community. He felt in two minds. He thoroughly enjoyed his work in the lift and his interactions with the residents, but it couldn't go on forever, could it? Later that evening he asked Pat if she could get a message to Michael about having a chat. The return message was that he was busy for a few days but would get back to Gabe as soon as he could.

It was a quiet time of day one very wet and blowy afternoon. Gabe knew that everyone who was out would not be back for a few hours and he made himself comfortable in the leather chair and pulled a book from the shelf. He had been making his way through the history books Ginny Cole had donated. He hadn't realised how little he knew about his own country's history. He had reached the Victorian period and he felt like he had a better grasp of this era. Just as he was deep into the death of Prince Albert he heard the outer door bang open. He wasn't sure if it was someone coming in or the wind catching it. He put his book aside and went to look.

As he entered the foyer Michael was there trying to furl an umbrella. "Ah Gabe, my boy. What a day! I've been blown here," he chuckled.

He leant the umbrella against the wall and shook off his waterproof coat.

"I'll put that in the laundry," said Gabe. "There's a place to hang wet washing if you don't want to use the tumble dryer."

He took the coat, which was heavy, and hung it up. By the time he returned to the lift Michael had ensconced himself in the armchair. "Well, Gabe. You told me about this, so I just had to come and see it for myself."

Gabe looked around the lift, as though seeing it for the first time. It was all a bit mismatched and, some might say, quirky, but there was a charm about it. Gabe smiled. "It works." He spread his hands to encompass it all.

Michael leant back and nodded gently. "So what do you need to see me about then, Gabe?"

Gabe explained about each of the residents and that he felt like the community had come together, "and so I wondered if I'd done what you wanted?"

Michael smiled and nodded again. "Yes, you've done very well, Gabe. Better than I expected, but I don't think you're quite there yet."

Gabe shrugged his shoulders. "So what else do I have to do?"

"I'm not sure, but I think you will know when it happens."

Gabe sat quietly. Part of him was reassured that what he was doing; or more accurately what the residents were doing, was what Michael had in mind. Part of him was troubled. What else could he do?

Michael seemed to read his thoughts. He leant forward with his hands clasped across his knees. "Don't think so hard about it, Gabe. You are doing wonderfully well, just let the moments happen."

Gabe nodded. If Michael thought he hadn't quite done enough yet there wasn't a great deal he could do or say.

Sensing his acceptance Michael rose from the chair, "Now I really must be off."

Gabe went and fetched Michael's coat. As he helped him into it Michael said, "You have done remarkably well, Gabe. Don't give up now."

Gabe watched as Michael picked up his umbrella and stepped out into the darkening weather, giving a final backward wave. Gabe signed, "Not quite there yet."

Chapter 48

The days were getting shorter and darker. His passengers were muffled up against the cold and the rain. Miss James and Captain Clive went out less and Sam had given up running to and from work. Only Robbie seemed unaffected by the changes until one afternoon.

"Gabe, Gabe." Robbie rushed into the lift, breathless. "Mr Groves said it's Christmas in a few weeks and we should try and do something special for someone else."

"Well, it's more like four weeks away, but yes, it would be good to do something for others."

"Well, I got this really brilliant idea while he was talking and I couldn't wait to come and tell you. We should have The Lift Book Club Christmas Party!" Robbie sat down with a thump, eyes bright and looked expectantly at Gabe.

"A Christmas Party? Here? In the lift?"

Robbie nodded enthusiastically. "We could ask each person to bring some food and share it all." Robbie noticed Gabe's hesitation, "We'd have to bring a few more chairs, but we could do it." The last part was almost a question.

Gabe nodded, slowly. "I think we need to invite everyone to a meeting to discuss it. Don't you? We'd have to work out when to have it because people are normally quite busy at Christmas, family and stuff."

Robbie's enthusiasm lifted on a new wave. "I'll write out some letters telling people about the meeting. We can do it tomorrow." With that, he left the lift and Gabe shortly afterwards heard the clatter of the closing flat door.

Later that evening, during the book club session, Robbie handed notes to Miss James, Captain Clive and Jenny. He then asked Gabe to take the lift to the floors to deliver to Sam and Mrs Cole.

"What does your mum think?" Gabe queried.

"She said it was a nice idea, but to see what the other residents say."

"I also think it's a lovely idea," said Miss James.

"Yes, young man. Good idea," chimed in the Captain.

Robbie beamed and winked at Gabe, "It's gonna be all right."

The next evening everyone turned up for the meeting, even Sam, who, fortunately, was between shift patterns. Everyone turned expectantly to Gabe who shook his head and said. "This is Robbie's idea, so he needs to chair this meeting."

Robbie nodded. He had come prepared. Sitting on his usual reading table were some pens and slips of blank paper. In his hand he held a sheet filled with writing. "I think it would be nice for everyone if we had The Lift Book Club Christmas Party."

General murmuring greeted this idea,

Robbie looked at his sheet of paper. "First we need to decide when to have it."

Ginny Cole and Sam clashed in their attempt to talk. Sam nodded to Ginny to go first. "I always go to a friend's for Christmas Day and Boxing Day afternoon Phil is coming over, so, if possible could we avoid those days?"

"And I always work Christmas Day," said Sam. "It's sort of a tradition that those staff who have younger children get the day off. So I wouldn't be able to make Christmas Day itself."

Robbie looked around to see if anyone else had something to say. Kathy Davies cleared her throat, she was obviously a little embarrassed. "Jenny will be going to her dad's the day after Boxing Day, so could we have it before Christmas?"

"How about Christmas Eve?" suggested Ginny. She looked first at Sam and then at Kathy, "would you be available the afternoon of Christmas Eve?"

Both nodded their heads. Robbie then looked at the Captain and Miss James who both nodded their agreement,

"Okay, Robbie? Christmas Eve afternoon?" Gabe asked. Robbie nodded and wrote something on his paper.

"Right, next, who wants to bring what food?" he said.

"Unless anyone has any objection could I make the Christmas Cake?" asked Ginny Cole. "The children could help with the 'stir up'."

Everyone nodded but Jenny asked, "What's a stir up?"

"It's when everyone who wants to has a stir of the cake mix and makes a wish for the year ahead," explained Ginny.

"Oh, yeh. I'd like that," said Robbie and Jenny nodded smartly.

Robbie turned to Alison, "Mum could you make your special trifle?" He turned to the rest of the company, "her trifles are brill."

Alison smiled and blushed and the others laughed. "Okay, Robbie. I'll do the trifle."

"Well," the Captain cleared his throat. "Ilene and I could make the sandwiches."

"That's an awful lot of sandwiches," said Sam, "How about I join you? Then there are three of us and I can ferry the plates around."

Robbie wrote on his sheet. "Jenny and I could make sausage rolls and butterfly cakes," said Kathy.

Robbie turned to Gabe. Now it was his turn to look embarrassed. "I, er, don't have access to a kitchen. Shall I buy some crisps and the makings for drinks?"

"That sounds an excellent idea," said Ginny swiftly.

"And we can use my tea set for the party," volunteered Miss James.

"Oh, no," chorused Kathy and Ginny. "What if it gets broken?" Kathy continued.

"It was made to be used. It's just sitting in my cabinet gathering dust. If anything gets broken, so be it. There are worse things happening in this world."

"Right," said Robbie, "so the next thing is can anyone bring extra chairs? We need two more."

"You can have my wicker one. Light. Easy to carry," said the Captain.

"I've got one that sounds similar," said Ginny. "You're welcome to use it."

"Right," said Robbie again. "The last thing is presents."

"Robbie!" his mum explained. "You don't ask for presents." She was very embarrassed.

"No, Mum. I've got this really great idea. Mr Groves said that his family either make the presents they give or they buy them from a Charity Shop and it mustn't be more than £5. We could do that."

There was a pause and then Sam said, "If we could add upcycling to the idea as well, I think that would be a good idea."

Gabe cleared his throat, "Could we also have the option to opt out? I don't want to receive any presents, or cards and I won't give any out."

Silence greeted this comment and then Robbie asked, "What's upcycling?"

"It's like what Gabe did with the bookshelves. He's turned something old into something new and different," explained Alison.

"I think if Gabe wants to opt out then he should be able to," said Kathy.

There were nods and noises of assent. Gabe still felt uncomfortable.

"All done," said Robbie. "I'll write on these bits of paper what each person said they'd do and give them to you later."

Apart from the book club participants, people were made to leave. As they were leaving Gabe said, "If we have the lift on the ground floor for the party we can use the little kitchenette in the laundry for anyone who wants to make tea and for the washing up."

"Good show. Bags the drying cloth," said the Captain as he left.

"Well done, Robbo, you handled that really well," said Gabe.

"Love the idea of homemade gifts or charity shop buys," said Ginny.

Chapter 49

Only a few days later Robbie again dashed into the lift calling for Gabe. "I've got this brilliant idea for upcycling but I need a grown-up to help. And you don't want a present so will you help me?" gushed from his mouth.

"Whoa! Calm down and explain."

Robbie peered out of the lift and checked the coast was clear. "I need empty bottles. Sort of wine bottles and things. Ones with really cool shapes or colours."

"Okay. And what are you going to do with them?"

"My friend says you can buy strings of lights, with a switch that looks like a bottle cork. And you can put these lights in the bottle and it looks pretty when you switch it on. Don't you think that would be a cool present?"

"Actually, that does sound good. So who would you do this for?"

"Well, anyone I can't find something for in the charity shops."

"And where are you planning to get the bottles from?"

"From the bottle bank on Wellsdene Walk. I thought if I went there on a Saturday, after football, I could ask people if I could put their bottles in the bank and check and see if there was some I'd like."

"It sounds like a good plan, but is your mum going to allow you to go there and hang around on your own?"

"Nah. I thought you could help. Tell Mum you would take me."

"There's a couple of problems with that, Robbo; and the most important is that I can't leave the lift unattended. I'm also not sure if your mum would be happy with you going out with me."

"You said you left the lift for an hour when you went and bought my map book." Robbie fixed Gabe with a steely glare. It was obvious that he had thought a lot about his plans and possible counterarguments.

Gabe looked at him and sensed his determination. "Okay. If your mum agrees I'll take you one Saturday. But only if your mum's okay with it."

"Thanks, Gabe. Mum's taking me to the Charity shops tomorrow night, after school, so I should know by Saturday how many bottles I need."

"What about the strings of lights. Where will you get them from?"

"Martin, he's my friend, he says the Pound Shop has sets of three for £1 so tomorrow I'll ask Mum if I can buy some sets. You know after the charity shops."

"Well, you sound like you've got it all planned. Let me know if we need to visit the bottle bank!"

Robbie gave him the thumbs up as he left the lift.

The next evening Robbie arrived with a carrier bag as well as his satchel. Without a word, he set it behind Gabe's chair and the normal proceedings of the book club carried on. At the end of the evening, Robbie said he wanted to ride the lift with Gabe whilst he dropped off the other book club members. Once everyone had left Robbie grabbed the carrier bag and began to empty it.

"Oh, it was killing me having to wait to show you what I found." Each item was carefully wrapped in bubble wrap or tissue paper. Reverentially Robbie unfurled blue paper from an object and held out his hand for Gabe to inspect.

Gabe picked it up. It was a leather camel, about fifteen centimetres from foot to the top of its hump. Brown leather with red cloth denoting the saddle and harness. A pair of beady eyes watched him. Gabe thought, 'this one would spit if it were alive!'

"For the Captain," said Robbie.

"Fantastic. This will remind him of his Morocco trip. Brilliant choice Robbo."

Next, he extricated a small china bowl from layers of protection. "It's Swanton ceramics, like Miss James has got. It's a sugar bowl. The lady said it was so cheap because it hasn't got its lid. But Miss James won't mind, will she?" There was a suggestion of uncertainty in his voice.

"Robbie, she'll love it. I can't think of a better gift. Well done again, mate."

The final object was wrapped in newspaper. Finally, Robbie found the centre and held it out to Gabe. It was a little pink glass bottle with a metal fairy sitting on the lid and her wings were also made of glass. "I thought Jenny might like that?" Definitely a question in his tone.

"It's superb. Can you fit a string of lights in there as well?"

"Oh, wow! I didn't think of that. Hang on. I put the lights in here as well." He burrowed into the bag and came out triumphantly waving a couple of boxes. He laid them on the desk for Gabe to see.

Gabe noted that one box contained four 'white light strings' and the other three 'coloured light strings'.

"What do yer think, Gabe? White or coloured?"

"Try the white first and then the colours."

Robbie did just that. He carefully removed the sitting fairy cap and fed in the string of lights. Gabe hunted in his pocket for a pen and gave it to Robbie to push the lights further in. Once completed Robbie switched them on.

Gabe had to admit they looked quite magical. Then Robbie tried the coloured string. Again very effective.

"What do you think?" Gabe asked.

"Um. The white looks nice coz the bottle is pink."

"Yes. That's what I thought. Will the fairy cap go on over the pretend cork?"

Robbie tried. It did. It was quite snug, but it did slip over.

"So, that's three presents sorted. So you've just got Sam, Mrs Davies, Mrs Cole, and of course, your mum." Gabe counted them off on his fingers. "Four."

Robbie shook his head. "Mum has an idea for Sam and it's going to be a joint present from me and Mum. So only three. But..." he tailed off.

"But?"

"I know what I want to get my mum. I saw it in the Heart charity shop. And its only £4. I've got the money, but I need to go to the High Street without Mum." He looked pleadingly at Gabe. "We could do that when we go to the bottle bank?"

Gabe's heart sank and he sighed. "Look, Robbie, I want to help. Honest. But the bottle bank is in the opposite direction from the High Street. We'd only manage one or the other in my break." Should he offer to give up a couple of lunchtimes? He didn't really have breaks. He was in the lift or he was at the hostel.

Robbie looked crestfallen. "My mum would say, concentrate on other people. But I really want to get this for her," he sighed deeply and dug a toe into the Persian carpet.

Gabe waited. He felt mean, but there had to be limits.

"Okay. We'll go and get my mum's present. I'll have another think about the bottles."

Carefully Robbie repackaged his objects and stowed them into the carrier. "Night Gabe," he called as he left.

"Night, mate."

Memoir of an Idiot

I felt really bad about making Robbie choose whether it was his mum's present or the bottle bank, so on my way home I stopped at the bottle bank. At that time of night, no one was about but someone had left a carrier bag of bottles on the side, rather than posting them through the slits. So I picked up the bag and began to deposit them. I held each one up to the street light to get an idea of shape and colour. Most were green wine bottles, but one was a clear, fat, stumpy shape, so I put that to one side. Another was tall and thin made from blue glass. Before coming back to my room tonight I knocked on the office door. Pat is normally there, and she was then. I explained about needing empty bottles and why and asked her if the hostel had a recycling bank for empties here.

Pat said, "Well, not so much a bank. Out back, we have a plastic bin where people are meant to put their glass. Don't know how full it is or how clean." She led me through to the back of the building, past the kitchen and dining room to a door into the back yard and pointed out a grey, plastic bin sat in one corner. "You're welcome to look through that."

The bin was on wheels so I wheeled it across to the light coming from the building. It felt about half full. I opened it and peered in but I couldn't see much. I thought my best bet was to empty it out and put back what I didn't want.

The clatter they made as I emptied it was loud and seemed to reverberate around the small yard tucked between tall buildings. I began to sort. Most of the bottles were small beer ones. Then I felt something larger. It was a whiskey bottle. Quite square in look, clear glassed. A few ridges. A bit different. I put it to one side and carried on putting small beer bottles back into the bin. Then I came across a really unusual shape. It was round based but flattened, made from green glass. I put that aside too. Once I'd finished clearing up I checked the two I'd set apart. There were no cracks or sharp lips. So that meant I have four bottles. I'll take all four so Robbie can make a choice about which ones he wants.

Chapter 50

The following day Gabe stored the recycling bottles behind his chair and waited for Robbie to let him know whether their trip to the High Street was on. It was a bright day, for a change, and, Gabe thought, ideal for a quick dash there and back in his lunch hour. Robbie appeared just after nine and assured Gabe that the trip to the High Street was fine by his mum.

"Right. I'll let the other residents know that the lift will be self-service. Shall we say 12 o'clock?"

"Yeh. Cool. Gabe, can I come and do some painting in here?"

"Painting? What kind of painting?"

"Mr Groves is getting the whole of Year 5 to think about recycling. And did you know that most Christmas wrapping paper you can't recycle?" Robbie rushed on before Gabe could reply. "It's because it's got glitter on, or metal bits or just too glossy."

"Okay. But how is that connected to you wanting to paint in here?"

"Mum bought me a roll of wallpaper. It's plain white. She says it's for lining the walls!" Robbie looked confused at this concept.

"Okay. Yeh, I know the sort of paper you mean, and…?"

"Well, I'm going to cut it into sections and use it for wrapping my Christmas presents in. But I need to decorate it first."

Dawning broke for Gabe. "Got you. Yes, you can paint in here… BUT…" he called before Robbie got too excited and dashed off, "you need to roll back the Persian rug and put down newspaper. Deal?"

"No problem, Gabe. Mum's got some newspapers. I'll go get everything."

"Hang on a second, Robbo. I've got something for you." Gabe reached behind his chair and gave Robbie the clanking carrier bag.

Mystified Robbie looked in. "Oh. Bottles." He pulled one out and then set the bag on the floor and pulled all four out and set them on the half-moon table to inspect. "Oh, thanks, Gabe. These are brill."

"I know you only need two but I thought if you had extras you could choose which ones to use."

"No, four is good, Gabe coz I thought I'd give one to Mr Groves as well."

"Perfect. Have you enough strings of light?"

"Yeh. But I might need some more for Mum's present. I'll show you when we go and get it."

"Okay. Take those home with you, then. Are you coming straight back with your painting stuff?"

"I've got to clean my teeth and make my bed, Mum says, before I can start my painting."

"Right. You go off and do that and I'll let everyone know that I'm out at lunchtime."

As Robbie left Gabe hit the button for the third floor. Sam was working so he just needed to check with Miss James and the Captain. It was a bright day, so they may well decide to go for a walk. On their floor, he knocked at the Captain's door. Gabe knew he was an early riser, so 9:30 was not going to cause any problems.

"Ah, Gabe. Morning. What can I do for you?"

"Morning, Captain. Just wanted to let you know that the lift will be self-service between twelve and one today. I wasn't sure if you and Miss James may be thinking of going for a walk, since it's dry for a change."

"Yes. We have just been planning such a thing. Out at ten, back by eleven, I should think. Just up to the cemetery."

"Well, it certainly is a bright day. Cold, but the wind is not too sharp," Gabe said as he returned to the lift. He waved to the Captain and pushed the button for the second floor. Gabe smiled to himself, he'd almost saluted the Captain, rather than wave, just now. Kathy Davies was working this Saturday, he knew. He'd waved off Jenny last night with John. Ginny Cole would probably be going out, she normally did on a Saturday. He knocked gently. He didn't think she was a late riser, but just in case. He needn't have worried Ginny appeared at the door already dressed for the outside.

"Morning Gabe. Everything all right?"

"Yes, fine. I am just letting residents know that I am off into the High Street at lunchtime."

"Oh, doing anything nice?" Then she blushed. "Oh, I'm sorry. That sounded nosey."

Gabe laughed. "No, it didn't. I'm taking Robbie to buy his mum's Christmas present. Apparently, he's seen what he wants to buy but needs his mum not to be around."

"Oh, how lovely. Well, as you can see, I'm off out as well. Old school friend. Would you believe we've been friends since we were both in infant school!"

"Wow," said Gabe. "I'm not even in touch with family who've known me that long."

Ginny laughed. "Hold the lift for me. I've just got to pick up my purse and keys."

She disappeared into the flat and Gabe wandered back to the lift. Merely seconds later Ginny joined him. "All set," she said as Gabe hit the bottom button.

On the ground floor, Robbie was waiting impatiently. He had built up a pile of stuff waiting to go into the lift. Ginny smiled and raised a quizzical eyebrow at Gabe. "Craft morning," said Gabe in explanation.

Ginny walked off waving. "What do you mean craft morning?" asked Robbie.

"I wasn't sure if you wanted to tell people that you were making your own wrapping paper. I thought you might have wanted it to be part of their Christmas present surprise."

Robbie thought, "Yeh. It should be a surprise."

"In that case, by all means, start preparing things but Miss James and the Captain will be coming down in a few minutes."

Robbie and Gabe set to preparing a space. Gabe carefully rolled back the rug, displaying the rough flooring below. Robbie scattered sheets of newspaper across it, making sure they overlapped so that the floor was covered again.

"While we're waiting for the Captain can we cut up the wallpaper?" asked Robbie.

Gabe unfurled a few feet. "How big do you want it? Most of your presents are quite small. If we make it square, would that be enough, do you think, Robbo?"

Robbie looked at the length Gabe had unrolled and gave it some deep thought. He then nodded.

"Scissors?"

Robbie darted outside the lift and brought in a bag. He rummaged through it and then triumphantly waved a pair of kitchen scissors. "Mum says only you are allowed to use these coz they're really sharp."

By eye, Gabe measured and cut seven pieces of paper. "That'll keep you going for now. I can always cut off more if you need it."

Just then the third floor called for the lift. "Perfect timing. Just put that bag in the corner, Robbo. I don't want Miss James falling over it."

As the lift doors opened Miss James looked surprised at the changes. "Mind how you go, Miss James. Robbie's doing some craftwork for school. There. Take a seat." Gabe led Miss James in and sat her in the armchair. The Captain took up his station by the doors.

"What's the craft, young man?" questioned the Captain.

Robbie looked blank and Gabe came to his rescue. "It's to do with recycling, isn't it Robbie?"

Robbie nodded, "Yeh, my teacher, Mr Groves, wants all of Year 5 to work on recycling."

Miss James nodded. "Very commendable."

"Miss James, while you're here can I pick your brains about something? You too, Captain?"

They both turned to look at Gabe enquiringly. "I had a thought and I wanted to run it past you. I am worried that Jenny may not have a present to give to her mum when we have our Christmas party. I am sure John will buy something for her to give to Kathy on Christmas Day, but I'm not sure he even knows about our party."

Miss James nodded. "That's very thoughtful of you, Gabe. Have you any ideas about what to do?"

Gabe shook his head. "I thought something to do with craft or upcycling, but I've no idea what."

They all three shook their heads. "We'll give it some thought, Gabe. A good walk gets the brains cells moving, I always find." With a cheery wave, the two left the lift and set off for their walk.

Chapter 51

Gabe was impressed with how much thought Robbie had obviously put into how to turn the wallpaper into wrapping paper and still be recyclable. He had several Christmassy templates; an angel, and stars in various sizes, some bauble shapes and Christmas trees. Using small pots of water-based paints as corner anchors Robbie laid out a sheet and then decided on a design. Carefully, he drew around the chosen templates and then painted them. Gabe was unsure about how good nine-year-olds were supposed to be with painting skills but Robbie seemed very good. He rarely went outside the lines and he kept his colours clear by using a different paintbrush in each colour.

At about ten fifty Gabe remarked, "The Captain and Miss James may be back soon. What do you want to do about your papers?"

Robbie looked up and then around the lift. He seemed surprised to see that every chair and floor space held a sheet of paper with a drying design. Gabe lifted one of the first ones Robbie had completed. "This one is dry," he touched another, "and this one." He stacked three of the sheets.

"That one is still wet." Robbie pointed to a fourth sheet. "I can see it's still shiny, and I've only just started this one." He looked down at the one on the floor by his knees.

"Okay. If you put that fourth one on top of these three dry ones and take them back to your flat. You just need to place the wet one somewhere to dry. And the one you've just started we can cover with some newspaper."

Robbie nodded and grabbed the stack of papers. Gabe heard him set them down as he used his key to get into his flat. Another bit of perfect timing Gabe thought as he laid the last covering over the fifth paper and heard the outer doors clang open. He peered out and, as he'd thought, the Captain and Miss James were returning.

"How was your walk?"

"It was good. Not too blowy but a breath of fresh air," said Miss James looking quite perky after her exercise. "I'm afraid I haven't come up with anything for Jenny, yet. But I'll put my thinking cap on."

The Captain, again took up guard by the lift doors. "Has Robbie finished his project?" he asked.

"Not quite. He's taken some of his work back to his bedroom."

"A good lad," said the Captain.

All three of them nodded their agreement.

Back on the ground floor, Robbie was waiting. In his hand nestled a pot of gold paint. "I want to use this for my mum's paper."

Gabe nodded and Robbie returned to his station on the floor. By 11:45, he had finished seven sheets of wrapping paper. The one for his mum Robbie had been painstaking in the extreme. Gold angels flew across a gold and white star-speckled sky.

"We need to get ready to set off for the High Street. What are we going to do with your mum's paper? It's still wet. Will you be able to smuggle it into your bedroom?"

Robbie shook his head pensively. "No. Mum'll see me," he looked around the lift as though seeking a hitherto unseen hiding place.

Gabe was also thoughtful and then he had an idea. "I know we'll use the laundry room. No one is going to use it today, so we should be fine." He lifted the sheet delicately by the corners and carried it to the laundry. A small table for piling your washing on whilst you began folding it was the perfect resting place.

Robbie nodded with approval.

Memoir of an Idiot

As promised I took Robbie to the High Street in my supposed lunch hour. It was a dashed affair. I set off at a smart pace and Robbie trotted along beside me. I knew that The Heart charity shop was about the middle of the street. We both arrived a little out of breath. Robbie pointed in through the window. "It's still there, Gabe," relief in his voice. "It's that glass heart thing."

I looked into the shop and on the counter next to the till was a heart-shaped glass bottle. I think it may have come from a cosmetic counter display in a large department store. Sort of a giant version of a scent bottle. It was about football size at its broadest point and had a collar of silver around the neck. I asked him what he thought his mum would do with it but he had it all planned. He was going to put strings of lights in it. I didn't want to dampen his enthusiasm but I thought it was going to need an awful lot of lights to fill it and what would he do with umpteen mock corks coming out of the neck. Robbie's face fell.

Then I had an idea. I knew that the Crystal Healing shop sells bags of mock crystals and beads. I didn't know how much they'd cost but they might go some way to fill up the bottle. I explained this to Robbie whose face lit up again.

Inside the shop, while Robbie counted out his money and asked for the glass heart, I happened to see a collection of bead necklaces. There were many shapes, sizes and colours. Suddenly I had a great idea. I chose four of the most interesting necklaces and took them to the cash desk. The lady was just beginning to wrap Robbie's gift when I realised we needed to know the size of the neck if we were buying stones or beads to go inside it. I used coins and found that a £1 coin was about the right size. To save us having to lug the bottle all the way to the Crystal place and back I asked the charity shop woman if she would keep hold of it while we dashed off. Once again I set the pace and Robbie kept up.

Crystal Healing was a typically alternative buying experience. As soon as we opened the door scents from incense candles and patchouli oil assaulted their noses. Robbie made a face.

The door chimes rattled as they closed the door. To one side was a display of gemstones. Robbie immediately gravitated to rose coloured stones in one tray. He liked the colour but not the cost so we wandered towards the back of the shop. A young man in a tie-dye T-shirt and a long dangly earring stepped out from a back room. I explained that my friend, Robbie was after some pearl-like or rose quartz like beads to go into the bottom of a glass bottle. I also said that he had loved the real deal but his Christmas money wasn't going to run to that. The young man was very helpful. He appeared to think and then beckoned Robbie over and pointed to bags of coloured glass beads in various shapes and sizes. Robbie went forward and handled the bags and picked out a bag of pearly pink stones and another of pearly silver. We made sure that they would fit the neck of the bottle, and they did but then it was a question of cost.

Robbie looked at each bag, they were 75p each. He then began to search all his pockets; his jeans, his jacket. Coin by coin was placed on the counter and it came to £1.20. I was in two minds about whether I should offer him the difference but thought that it was important that he did this on his own.

Robbie looked wistfully from one bag to the other. He held them up to the light. He fingered the bags, feeling the stones through the plastic. He was very torn. The young man asked what Robbie wanted them for and he explained about the bottle and the lights and needing to fill the bottom a bit.

The young man looked thoughtful and then leant towards Robbie and spoke conspiratorially. He claimed that the bags were going to be in a sale next week and that if Robbie promised not to tell anyone he would sell them today at the sale price. Of course, Robbie was delighted and even swore an oath that he wouldn't tell anyone. Money changed hands and Robbie slipped the bags of stones into his jacket pocket.

As we left Robbie called back, "Thank you and Merry Christmas." I also looked back and mouthed "thank you." The young man gave me the thumbs-up sign. It made me think again about the kindness of strangers.

Chapter 52

That weekend Robbie spent a lot of time in the lift. Gabe had agreed to keep his mum's glass heart in the lift behind the armchair and Robbie decided the lift was also the perfect place for making and wrapping his gifts, with Gabe on hand for extra help. The homemade wrapping paper worked really well and Robbie and his mum had made gift tags out of last year's Christmas cards.

Robbie decided that Mrs Cole should have the blue bottle with white lights and Mrs Davies should have the square clear one with coloured lights. That left him both white and coloured lights for his mum's glass bottle. The problem was: what to do with the pretend cork switches. One would fit into the neck but that still left two hanging outside. In the end, Gabe taped all three ends together in a line and attached them to the back of the collar on the neck. From the front, they were barely visible.

While Robbie busied himself with construction, Gabe was busy with destruction. Using the scissors Robbie had brought in for cutting string and tape Gabe destroyed the necklaces. He clipped the string holding them in place and emptied the separate parts into the paper bag they had been wrapped in.

Several times Robbie looked across at Gabe, clearly curious as to what he was doing and why. Eventually, he could contain himself no longer. "Why're you breaking them necklaces?"

"I thought if we got some string, or maybe thin elastic, Jenny could design her own necklace for her mum. What'd you think?"

Robbie contemplated the idea and peered in the bag at all the shapes and colours. "Cool!"

A seal of approval, Gabe thought.

By Sunday afternoon Robbie's presents were ready. "Can I leave them behind the armchair, please Gabe?"

"Okay. When are you giving them out?"

"I thought at the Lift Book Club Christmas Party?"

"That's fine. Are people going to be allowed to open them then? It won't be Christmas proper."

Robbie mulled that idea over before saying, "Yeh! I want to see them open their presents."

Robbie was not the only one thinking deeply about Christmas presents and all seemed to have taken on board the charity, homemade or upcycling idea. Ginny Cole came in from a shopping expedition one afternoon obviously delighted in her purchases. "Do you know, Gabe? You can get some lovely things in charity shops. And some of it is practically new!" She swung her bag onto the seat of the armchair and hunted inside. "Look at this." In her hand, she held a ship in a bottle with a little wooden stand. "Do you think the Captain will like it?"

"I think he'll love it. How very appropriate. Any other goodies?"

"Well, I did come across this, and again she hunted in her bag until she found and brought out a box."

From where he was Gabe couldn't make out the contents and put out his hand for a closer look. On inspection, it was a kit for making a Roman centurion. Complete with shield and spear. Reading the contents list he saw glue, paints and brushes were supplied. "Robbie?"

Ginny nodded.

"Well, judging from his skills with a paintbrush I think this will suit him down to the ground."

Ginny smiled broadly. "Do you know? I think this is the most fun I've had Christmas shopping in a long while. It had become a bit of a chore. But I'm really enjoying myself."

The Captain and Miss James were also accepting the challenge for the Christmas presents. Each morning they took a gentle stroll to the High Street. "When we get there," Miss James explained, "we go our separate ways so we don't know who's buying what. It's quite exciting," she giggled like a young girl. They were both getting a great deal of enjoyment from it. Miss James confessed on one of her, now rare, solo journeys,

"It's been a while since I've had anyone to buy for, for Christmas or birthdays, come to that. I'd forgotten the pleasure of anticipation. You know, will they like it." Gabe nodded. "Miss James, I think I've come up with an idea for Jenny making her mum a present," he explained about the beads.

"A superb idea. And do you know, I've got some silver elastic cord. I'm sure it would be thin enough for those beads. I'll bring it out for you. I haven't been this excited about Christmas since I don't know when."

Gabe noted there was quite a gleam in her eyes when she said this.

"But, Gabe. I want to ask your opinion. I've been thinking about giving Robbie a piece of my Swanton ware. What do you think?"

"He was delighted with the plates he received when he visited the factory. But do you want to break up your sets?"

"I'd thought about that and I thought I'd give him one of the commemorative jugs they made. I've got several. Some mark the Queen's coronation and jubilees. Others mark things like D-Day. But I was thinking about giving him the one that marked the 200th anniversary of Etherington's Ceramics?"

Gabe smiled broadly. "I can't think of anything he'd like more. It will be a lovely memento of many things in one gift."

Miss James returned the smile and sat with a beautiful look on her face as Gabe returned her to the third floor.

Memoir of an Idiot

I've re-read what I have written so far and it seems to me that I have described events but that it lacks passion. The trouble is when I look back I only see what I did through my eyes, not those of other people. So, Michael, if you read this, it's not that I don't know how bad I was, it's just that at the time that was how it was. That was how I felt.

The work with Dirk went into a second week and then on Friday, I saw through the window that a young woman was serving at the counter. I didn't go in. Dirk was paying me daily so I didn't need to go and say goodbye. I had a little money left, although, in retrospect, an awful lot had gone on the bags. Dirk had fed me as well as paying for my time, he'd also suggested that I go across to the barber's and get a haircut and shave in exchange for a couple of bacon sarnies. In many ways, I was in the best shape I'd been in for a while. Unfortunately, my mind did not immediately move on to getting another job and so it wasn't long before I was back to looking for a means of making money. Smike put me in touch with a guy who ran a group that nicked copper wire from building sites. I only did the one job but I was scared out of my wits. My hands shook so badly I didn't get half as much copper wire as the others but I got enough for my next bag.

Chapter 53

Sam was a little less sanguine about the gift buying and also asked for Gabe's advice.

"Gabe, when I was in sixth form, we had to take a 'recreational topic' for a Wednesday afternoon. I chose pyrography. At the time, I got quite good at it, but I haven't done any for ages, but I do still have my pyrography pen." He paused, and Gabe waited. "I noticed, at work, there is a stall that sets up by the canteen, twice a week. It's run by the Friends of the hospital. I noticed that they're selling wooden boxes. All different sizes and prices. It's all for charity, so it's like a charity shop. Do you think people would like them if I then burnt in their name or a design or something?" He looked hopefully at Gabe.

"I think that something you have put time and effort into will be appreciated by everyone. And the fact that you can personalise them will be an added bonus."

Gabe hesitated, before continuing. "Please say if I'm out of order, but you're a Muslim, aren't you?"

Sam nodded.

"So do you celebrate Christmas?"

Sam laughed. "Not in the same way you do. We believe that Jesus was a prophet and we venerate him in our teachings. And his Mother, Mary, but we don't celebrate his birthday. It's part of the reason I don't mind working on Christmas Day."

"But what about all this present giving?"

"If I was at home or with another Muslim household, we would not be celebrating, but I can choose to join you in your celebrations. It just doesn't mean the same thing to me."

"I'm not sure the Jesus part resonates with very many people that are supposed to be Christian, if I'm honest."

"No. But for some, it is still very important and I can respect that."

"Thanks. You didn't mind me asking, did you?"

"No. If you don't ask how will you know? More people should be asking questions."

A few days later Gabe got a call from the third floor and it was Sam. He peered into the lift to check that Gabe was alone before pulling from behind his back an oblong box. He handed it to Gabe. "What do you think? Please be honest if you think it's not good enough."

Gabe took the proffered box. It was a pencil box with a lid that pivoted on a screw at one end. The top was covered in a design of fairies and flowers in shades of burning. Gabe was amazed. "This is fantastic. I didn't know you could get such a variation in the colours when you burnt the wood. This must have taken you hours."

Sam smiled and glanced down. If he blushed Gabe was unable to see but he was obviously pleased with the praise.

"The hardest part is getting a design you like and transferring it onto the wood. The burning part is easy."

Gabe thought that last part was probably untrue. The depth and change of colour achieved just by burning the wood was incredible.

"The stall where I bought the boxes also sells activity books so I invested in a couple of adult colouring books. You know the ones called things like 'Colouring for Zen!' Sam laughed. "But they do have some lovely designs."

"So, is that box for Jenny?"

"Yeh. I thought she's of the age where fairies are still real and I noticed a few weeks ago at the book club she was reading about fairies that looked after the flowers."

"So, a perfect design," Gabe agreed.

"Yeh. That's what I thought."

Neither Alison nor Kathy approached Gabe about present hunting, but Robbie said his mum was making all the presents and he was helping. Gabe was eager to discover what these gifts could be. The only hint Robbie would give was that the book club would find them useful.

Gabe was worried that Kathy might find present buying for everyone a financial burden in her new situation. Jenny had been surprisingly mute on the subject, but like Robbie, she insisted that she was helping with the making of the presents. Gabe had asked her during one of the book club sessions whether she was going to make a present for her mum. She looked a little bemused and Gabe explained his idea. She was delighted. The next session Miss James brought the silver cord and estimated the length they would need for a necklace. Gabe emptied the beads onto the half-moon pie crust table, its rim keeping them from rolling off. Jenny ran her fingers through the beads and began to separate them out. Gabe wasn't sure what the criteria was but Jenny seemed to know what she was doing.

When she began to thread them they hit a problem. Although the cord would go through the holes in the beads, it wasn't coming out the other end. "I think we need something solid and straight to tie the cord to," said Gabe.

"We need to make an aiglet," said Miss James.

Four pairs of enquiring eyes swung her way. She laughed. "You know that plastic bit on the end of shoelaces so they're easier to thread through the eyes."

"Never knew they were called that," said the Captain.

"I think we could use some tape and create an aiglet," continued Miss James.

"Got you," said Gabe. "Robbo would you nip back home and bring back that tape you were using to stick your paper, please?"

Robbie scampered off. Within a minute he was back, holding out the tape. Gabe set to making the aiglet.

"Squash it to a point," said Miss James, "A bit like a needle."

The aiglet was a complete success and Jenny made her mum a necklace. Although Gabe could discern no obvious pattern there was a beauty to the way Jenny had marshalled the beads and everyone agreed it was splendid.

Miss James found some tissue paper to wrap it in and agreed to look after it for Jenny until the party.

Chapter 54

The week of the party arrived. Jenny and Robbie had finished school and were wired with excitement. Miss James and Gabe offered to have them for extra book club sessions and Miss James taught them how to make paperchain decorations. Robbie also had the idea of using his wallpaper lining and his templates to make things hang from the chains.

Gabe was pleased with how thoughtful Robbie was with Jenny. Allowing her to colour her angels and stars any way she wanted. Gabe had feared Robbie would want them done a specific way or moan if Jenny coloured outside of the lines, but he didn't. He was encouraging and admired her handiwork. Enormous piles of chains grew in the corners of the lift until Gabe decided that the best thing would be to put them up, ready for the party. Fortunately, the age of the lift meant that the structure was wooden and tacks were easy to use.

Gabe borrowed a step ladder from Alison and Robbie acted as his safety officer. Jenny and Miss James sorted out the lengths of chain and decided which ones went where and what needed to be hanging on them. They had such an extensive stock of decorations that Gabe even allowed an overflow into the foyer.

Miss James and the Captain also put on extra film club afternoons. After one such afternoon, Gabe noticed that Robbie was very thoughtful on his way home.

"Everything all right, mate?"

Robbie shook himself. "Yeh. We just watched this really old, old film. It was in black and white it was so old. It was about an angel called Clarence and he had to help a man so that he could get his angel's wings. Do you believe in angels, Gabe?"

Gabe sat and thought. The lift doors had opened but Robbie hadn't made a move to leave. He waited. "Umm. I think I do." Gabe nodded, more to himself than Robbie. "You find angels in lots of different cultures, not just in the bible. And I suppose if when we die we go to heaven or hell, those who go to heaven must need to prove they're angel material. So, yeh. I think I do believe in angels."

Robbie nodded. "And do you think a bell rings when an angel gets his wings?"

"To be honest, Robbo. I've never really thought about it. I know the film, it's Jimmy Stewart in 'It's a Wonderful Life'. It was one of my Gran's favourite films. We'd watch it every Christmas. It was always on the TV. I'd like to think that there's some kind of recognition when an angel gets his wings, so, yeh, why not a tinkling bell?"

This seemed to satisfy Robbie and he left the lift. He then popped his head back through. "Oh, sorry, Gabe, nearly forgot. Miss J says can you pop up and collect something from her flat."

"Miss J?"

Robbie shuffled his feet. "Well, saying Miss James every time seems a lot and she likes it when I call her Miss J. She told me," the last was said in a tone of slight defiance.

"That's fine. As long as she's okay with it. Thanks, Robbo. I'll go up now."

On the third floor, Miss James' door was open. Gabe knocked, walked in and called, "Miss James. It's Gabe."

Her voice came from her sitting room. "In here Gabe." As he entered the room, she said, "Thanks for coming up. I just thought that we may need a few more tables in the lift when we have the party."

Gabe nodded. "That's probably a good idea. I was wondering where we were going to put everything."

"So I had a thought. In my alcove, I have a little fold-up table. It matches the chairs you've already got. But I've also got a fold-up pasting table."

Gabe raised an eyebrow.

"Yes, I know." She smiled. "Why I didn't get rid of it when I moved in here, I don't know. And having arrived it's just sat there," she stopped as though trying to remember her thought processes back then. She continued. "I thought we could cover it. I have a lovely large tablecloth and we could use it to lay the food out on. Then we can use your little table and mine for people to rest cups and plates on. Does that sound like a plan?"

"It does indeed, Miss J." Gave caught himself. "Sorry, Miss James. I've just been talking with Robbie."

"No sorry necessary. I rather like being Miss J. It's friendlier. But not too friendly!" She smiled again. "So, on the morning of the party will you come and collect my two tables, Gabe?"

"Of course, I will. This is shaping up to be a great event."

Chapter 55

Robbie was out in the foyer waiting for Gabe's arrival on the morning of the party. "Come on, Gabe. We've got lots to do."

"Hold your horses, Robbo. Let me get my coat off and hang it in the laundry and then we'll make a plan of campaign."

Robbie danced alongside him as he headed for the laundry. "Mum's made two trifles. She wasn't sure one would be enough. She made them last night. She says she's just got to put the sprinkles on, but she can't do that yet, otherwise they bleed. How can they bleed Gabe?" Robbie stopped. Coming up for air.

"I think she means that the colours will melt a bit and stain the cream."

Gabe wasn't sure he even heard the answer before he was off on his next breathless speech.

"Miss J says we can go and collect the tables any time after nine. It's after nine, Gabe, so we could do that first. The Captain says you can have his chair anytime you like. I don't know about Mrs Cole's though."

Gabe returned to the lift, placed a heavy bag on the floor and sat down. He pointed to the armchair and made Robbie sit. "Right we need to make a plan. What order we need to do things in."

Robbie fidgeted, just wanting to start doing anything.

"If we collect Miss J's tables first." Robbie smirked at Gabe's use of Miss J. "And the tablecloth. We can set that up in here, ready for when people want to bring out the food. Yes?"

Robbie nodded.

"We also need to collect her tea service and put the plates on the table and set the cups and saucers up in the laundry kitchenette."

"Okay. Come on let's go!"

Miss James was all ready for them. The tea service was already wrapped and in a box. "I thought it would make it easier for moving."

Gabe lifted the box and took it to the lift. He was surprised at how heavy it was. By the time he'd returned Robbie had already manhandled the small fold up table out but the paste table was proving too big for him.

"Okay, Robbo. You take that table to the lift and I'll try and get the big one out." Robbie trotted off and was soon back. Gabe had secured a hold on the paste table and pulled it around the boxes and out into Miss James' hall.

"Right, mate. Can you take the other end?"

Robbie lifted the other end. It was obviously heavy for him but he was determined to do his part. Once the table was in the lift he blew out a puff of air. "Phew. That's heavy."

Gabe nodded his agreement. He was just about to press for the ground floor when he heard Miss James call. "Robbie. Don't forget the tablecloth."

Robbie dashed out and came back carrying a large white cloth draped across his outstretched arms.

On the ground floor, Gabe carried the box of tea service to the kitchenette. "Robbie, do you think you could manage to unwrap the tea service and set out the cups and saucers? You need to be very careful."

"I can do it. I'll be extra 'specially careful. I know Miss J loves these."

Gabe went back to the lift and set up the paste table along one side. He had to move up the bookshelf, but otherwise, it was a good fit. He unfurled the tablecloth. It was snowy white, but with gold stars sprinkled across it. Very festive.

He returned to Robbie, who, true to his word, had very carefully unwrapped the tea service. The set was beautiful. A cluster of small red roses were the main design but with gold rims on the plates, saucers and teacups. The cups also had gold lines defining their handles. Robbie was handling them with reverence.

Gabe picked up the plates and bowls. Robbie followed him. "My mum has brought some Christmas paper serviettes. I'll go and get them. And she said she can give us the spoons for the trifle." As he was dashing off, Gabe called. "Robbie, can you ask your mum if she's got some bowls I could put my crisps in, please?"

"Yeh. Okay."

Robbie returned in less than ten minutes with a selection of plastic bowls in various colours and sizes. He gently laid them on the table. Then with a clatter, he let slip a handful of spoons. "Here you go, Gabe. And Mum says I've got to put serviettes between the plates."

As Gabe emptied crisps into bowls Robbie delicately laid serviettes between the plates. The design on the serviettes was playful; Santa and Rudolph having a snowball fight! They each finished their task at about the same time.

"Robbie, do you think your mum would have room in her fridge for this carton of milk? I'm worried it'll go off if it gets too warm."

"Yeh, I should think so." He grabbed the milk and disappeared. Gabe took the rest of the tea making stuff to the kitchenette. They met back at the lift. "All done?"

Robbie nodded. "What's next?"

"I think if we go and get the extra chairs from the Captain and Mrs Cole, we can leave them in the foyer until we want to use them."

Chapter 56

At the Captain's flat sandwich production was in full swing. They had a kind of conveyor belt approach to the process. The Captain was at one end of the table, buttering rounds of bread. These he passed on to Miss J who was filling them with all sorts of goodies. When filled she passed them onto Sam who was cutting them into triangles and arranging them on plates and platters. Someone had even gone to the trouble of putting a little bit of lettuce on the plates and a doily to enhance the appearance.

Gabe and Robbie entered through the open door. "All right for us to take your spare chair, Captain?" Gabe asked.

"Yes. Of course. Robbie, you know which one." The Captain waved his buttery knife around. "All ship shape and well managed here."

"I can see that. The table is up and ready in the lift as soon as you want to bring them in."

"It's nice and cool in here," said Miss James, "so we'll cover them over and bring them in just after lunch. Does that fit in with everyone's plans?"

"Fine. We'll be back for them later. Come on Robbie show me which chair we need to take."

Gabe lifted the chair out and Robbie guided and held doors open. Having placed the chair in as far as it could go they stopped on the second floor. Ginny Cole was ready for them. "I've moved the chair to the hall. So it's all ready for you."

"Thanks, Miss," said Robbie. Again he guided Gabe and the chair to the lift. Ginny called out. "Can I also bring the cake out now?"

Having squeezed the second spare chair in Gabe called out, "We'll take these chairs down first and then come back for it."

"Okay. See you in a minute."

On their return to the second floor, Ginny was holding a large round Christmas cake and a knife. Gabe could see the strain of holding it on her face and instantly took it from her. "I can't believe how heavy that cake is. I hope that doesn't bode ill for the taste," she half laughed.

Once the cake was on the table Robbie oohed and aahed. Ginny was a very proficient cake decorator. The cake was a scene of skating penguins and reindeer. Some were skating gaily round a blue circle, whilst others were just showing their heads or their feet as they had ploughed into snowdrifts.

"That's brill, Miss."

"He's right. That's very clever and very funny."

"Thank you," she did blush a little. "I hope it tastes good."

Chapter 57

The table was full. Groaning may have been a more accurate term as Gabe noticed a slight bowing in the middle. The chairs were full and the extra ones had been pulled up to the lift's doors. Jenny was on her footstool, and Robbie had joined Sam on his beanbag. Gabe and Alison had made cups of tea and ferried them through to the lift. Now Robbie was handing around plates of sandwiches and sausage rolls. Gabe noted that he went to Miss J first, then the Captain and then his mum. Before handing them around more broadly.

Through half-full mouths, compliments were made about the food. "Oh, chicken and mayo, one of my favourites. Is that black pepper with it?"

"These sausage rolls are wonderful. Is this your own pastry?"

"I love the pickle in with the cheese. What is it?"

"Where did you get the sausage meat? Lovely."

Replete with the savoury section they moved on to the trifle and butterfly cakes. "I made the butterflies," Jenny said proudly.

"They're lovely," said Robbie cramming a whole one in his mouth.

"Robbie!" exclaimed his mum.

For a second he looked abashed, but everyone else was smiling and he soon smiled as well, once the cake was swallowed.

After the sweet Robbie declared. "I think it's present time now. Then we can have some Christmas cake."

"I've got to pop back to the flat to collect my presents," said Alison. "One was too big to wrap."

Everybody waited until she returned, continuing the compliments about the food and the entire idea of having the Lift Book Club Christmas Party. When Alison returned, it was obvious what one of the gifts was and who it was for and so she began the present giving proceedings. "This is for you, Sam." It was a multi-coloured beanbag. Each face of the bag was a different primary colour and each seam was covered with a braid made form the two adjacent colours.

"I remember you saying your flat needed some colour and that even your beanbag was boring!" explained Alison a little bashfully.

"This is stunning. I might well donate my old beanbag to The Lift Book Club. Thank you, both, very much."

"I made the braid and filled it with polystyrene balls," said Robbie proudly.

"Where did you learn to braid so well?" asked Sam.

"Oh, it's was when I went to the summer school. They showed us how to do friendship bracelets."

"And Robbie also contributed his braiding skills to the rest of the gifts." Alison handed round small packages to the others. They were bookmarks. Homemade bookmarks and Robbie's braiding skills created the tail for them. Everyone exclaimed with delight.

"Well, since we're a book club, I thought bookmarks were good," said Robbie.

"Very good," said Miss James.

"I'll give mine out now," continued Robbie. He turned a serious face to Sam. "Me and Mum made your present and coz it's so big I didn't think you'd want another present from me."

Others in the lift tried to prevent grins from appearing. Sam maintained a perfectly serious face, "That's quite right, Robbie. No worries."

Both Miss J and the Captain had to wipe their eyes when they saw what Robbie had bought them. The Captain blew his nose loudly and said, "My Morocco days."

Miss J said, "Oh, Robbie, it's lovely. I don't have a sugar bowl. Now I can use this one."

Robbie beamed, pleased with himself and their response. Then he gave out the other gifts, all except his mum's. When people realised that the paper was hand-decorated and Robbie's reasoning behind it, they were very impressed. Ginny Cole was the first to discover the switch for the lights and all were delighted. Jenny especially liked her pink bottle and fairy. Then it was Alison's turn. Robbie held out his bundle, inexpertly wrapped round such a difficult shape. "To the best Mum, ever!"

Everyone looked on as she undid the wrapping and displayed her heart-shaped glass. Robbie showed her how to switch it on and Gabe had to marvel at how the lights reflected off the coloured pebbles. It really did look quite magical.

Alison did cry. She hugged Robbie tightly until he wiggled for release. "Robbie, I think this is the best present ever."

Gabe was aware that paper was piling up and offered to go to the kitchenette. "I bought some black sacks. Give me any empty cups and I'll give them a rinse and we can have tea and cake later. Cups were passed and Gabe carried several at one time with his fingers through the handles. They arrived safely in the sink. Gabe began to run hot water and gave a squirt of the washing-up liquid. He'd forgotten to bring a teacloth. Well, in fact, he didn't have a teacloth. He'd ask Alison when he went back."

He almost dropped the first cup he was rinsing when a voice said. "Ah, Gabe. How are you doing?" It was Michael.

Chapter 58

"Did they see you?" Gabe nodded towards the lift and the party.

"No, I don't think so. They were all too busy swapping and enjoying presents."

Gabe felt relieved. He wasn't sure why. He didn't want to have to explain Michael to them.

"They seem to be having a wonderful time, Gabe."

"Yeh. I think they are. All sorts of friendships have been born, and between what would seem, the unlikeliest people. They are a lovely group of people."

Michael nodded. "They are. And they are a happier group of people."

Gabe went to interrupt but Michael held up his hand. "I know some of them still have difficulties in their life, but they are succeeding and today they are happy. No one can be happy all of the time. But I do sense a deep contentment from some of your residents."

Gabe shrugged. What was he supposed to say: 'Yeh. It's all because of me'? But it wasn't. It was all because of them. Each and every one of them had given of themselves to the others and in doing so had made something really special. It didn't need him.

"Do you think I am finished here now?" Gabe wasn't sure he wanted a positive answer.

"Let's go and watch the finish of the present giving, shall we?"

They held back from the lift doors but could see most of the people in the lift and hear everyone. It was Jenny's turn to give out presents. Her mum had made handkerchiefs; large ones for the men and dainty ones for the ladies. Even Robbie had a set. Jenny had cut the ribbon and tied the hankies together, making neat bows. Having given out the last one to the Captain, who immediately proceeded using one of them to wipe his eyes, Jenny turned to Miss James. Reaching into her handbag she gave Jenny the tissue-wrapped gift for her mum.

"I made this for you, all by myself," she said proudly, handing her mum the package.

"Oh, my goodness." Kathy was tearful even before she unwrapped her necklace. There were oohs of admiration from the others as Kathy pulled it over her head. From where he stood Gabe thought it looked lovely.

"A good plan, that," Michael said quietly.

Then it was Sam's turn to give out his boxes. They weren't wrapped, just tied with bows. Robbie and Jenny both had pencil boxes. Gabe couldn't see what the design was for Robbie's but he was delighted with it, "Mum, look. It's a pirate ship, and look, there's a treasure map that goes onto the bottom."

The others were equally admiring of their boxes. Miss J kept running her fingers over the design and the Captain explored it in great detail. Ginny said, "Did you do the pyrography, Sam?"

Gabe couldn't hear his reply but Ginny continued. "You know you could do this for real. People would pay good money for something so intricate and individual and so well executed."

Other voices agreed with her.

"In answer to your question, Gabe. Yes, I think you're finished here."

"When do I have to go?"

"I think tomorrow. Are you going to say goodbye?"

Gabe thought, then shook his head. "No, too much explaining. I'll leave a letter to Robbie."

Michael went to interrupt, but it was Gabe's turn to hold up his hand. "I won't go into details. I'll just say goodbye and leave him a gift. I brought it with me today and was going to give it to him at the end of the party. But I think I will leave it for him tomorrow."

"Well, when you have finished here come to HQ and we'll get you fitted up for your uniform. You should be very proud of yourself, Gabe."

Gave shook his head and waved towards the lift, "No, you should be proud of them."

Michael nodded, whether in agreement or with sympathy. Gabe tried a last bid, "Do I have to go now? Could I stay a few months more?"

This time the look on Michael's face was definitely one of sympathy. "Sorry, Gabe. This was your second chance, but it was only ever going to be for a set time. You don't belong here anymore."

Gabe nodded slowly, still watching the residents, his friends. Michael quietly stepped around the lift and waved to Gabe from the outer doors. In a stage whisper, he said, "See you later. Remember tomorrow, when you come back you must be in civvies."

Chapter 59

Gabe returned to the kitchenette to wash the cups. A few minutes later Alison appeared with a few more. "There you are, Gabe. You okay?"

Gabe smiled easily. "I'm fine. Just thinking about what lovely people you all are."

Alison smiled too, "I think it is you who has brought it out of us. Lots of disparate lives pulled together by a lift that looks like something from a fairy tale. Thank you, Gabe."

Gabe shrugged the compliment off. "All down to you and the people in there." To change the subject, he asked, "Does anyone want another cup of tea? Would you go and ask?"

Later, with more cups of tea consumed and Ginny Cole's Christmas cake cut and devoured, the party mellowed into a comfortable daze. Even the children were content to lie on the Persian rug looking up at their decorations. Eventually, Sam made a move. "Sorry, everyone, but my shift starts at six tomorrow morning so I need my sleep. Can I do anything before I disappear?"

"Could you help me wash, dry and rewrap Miss James' tea service?" asked Alison.

"Sure. No problem," he said readily.

"You'll need a teacloth, Alison. I didn't have one," Gabe said.

"Okay. Sam, and Robbie, you can help too. You start to take the tea things into the kitchenette and I'll pop home for a teacloth."

Ginny also got up. "And everyone needs to take home a chunk of Christmas cake. I can't be left with so much." She took up the knife, looked around at the residents, counting to herself, and began to cut large slices. Using spare serviettes she wrapped each piece and began to hand them out.

There were a few cakes, sandwiches and sausage rolls left. Miss James said, "I'm happy to take back the sandwiches. If anyone wants to join the Captain and me tomorrow afternoon to watch the Queen, you're welcome to join us, aren't they Roger?"

"Yes, indeed. My Flat, Just before three."

"In that case do you want to take all the leftover food?" asked Kathy. "Jenny and I would love to join you tomorrow afternoon."

"Good idea," said the Captain.

Within minutes the food was rewrapped and once all the tea service was in the kitchenette Gabe took the lift to the third floor. A little train of helpers carried the food to the Captain's fridge.

"If you don't mind I think I'll get out here too," said Miss James. "I feel exhausted with merriment!"

"Okay, Miss J. I'll leave your tables in the lift when they're clear and we'll sort them out later. I'll just bring your presents in for you."

"Thank you, Gabe. What a lovely afternoon." Slowly, she made her way along to her flat with Gabe in attendance. "Do you know this has been a wonderful day? I even enjoyed the sandwich making!" She laughed to herself.

Gabe followed her into her flat and laid her presents in the chair by the window. Miss James was already heading for her bedroom. "Good night, Miss J and Merry Christmas."

"Merry Christmas to you, Gabe," she called over her shoulder.

On the next trip down, they found the washing up was still being done and so they loaded the two spare chairs into the lift. On the third floor, Gabe and Ginny moved the wicker chair back into the Captain's main room.

"Capital! Thank you. Might take a nap now. Lovely afternoon. Merry Christmas to you."

"Merry Christmas!" was chorused back.

On the second floor, they offloaded Ginny's chair. "Is there anything more that needs doing, Gabe?"

"No. I'll collapse the two tables Miss J loaned us and put them, her tablecloth and box of crockery in the corner for tomorrow."

"Thank you, Gabe. A lovely party."

"Not my idea. This is all down to Robbie."

"Merry Christmas Gabe."

"Merry Christmas Ginny."

Kathy and Jenny had already gone into their flat but as Gabe walked past the door Kathy called, "Gabe, Wait." She appeared from the flat, "just wanted to say, thank you. And Merry Christmas."

Jenny appeared from behind her, "Merry Christmas Gabe."

"Merry Christmas to you both and I hope the New Year brings all that you hope for."

He waved as they stood in their doorway and the lift doors closed.

In the kitchenette, he found Sam and Alison in conversation as Robbie wrapped the last of the plates. Gabe heard her say, "You're welcome to join us on Boxing Day. We don't do much. Perhaps take a walk in the afternoon if the weather is good."

"Thanks. I'll bear that in mind. Can I let you know tomorrow evening when I get off shift?"

"Of course. Are you done, Robbie?"

"Yeh."

"Yes, you mean?"

"Yes. All carefully wrapped. Oh, hello Gabe. Do you want to take this up to Miss J?"

"Thanks, Robbo. I'll leave it in the lift. Miss J has gone for a rest."

"Is she all right?" Robbie looked worried.

"She's absolutely fine, but she's not used to this much excitement and noise. I don't know how old she is, but things like that can make older people very tired. I think the Captain was heading for a nap as well."

"I don't blame them." Sam yawned and stretched. "I'd better get to bed too. That 4:30 alarm is going to come far too soon. I'll take the box, Gabe." He held the box in his arms and followed Gabe to the lift. Gabe showed him where to place it and topped it off with the tablecloth.

"That's all Miss J's things," Gabe pointed. "In case she wants them back in before I'm here again."

"Okay, Gabe. I can sort them. Hope you have a Merry Christmas."

"Merry Christmas to you too."

"Night, Gabe." Sam gave a friendly wave as he left.

Back on the ground floor, Robbie and Alison were waiting. "Hello, everything all right?"

"I just wanted to say Merry Christmas, Gabe."

"Thank you and Merry Christmas to you too."

"It's been a wonderful afternoon, Gabe. Thank you for everything."

"As I keep reminding people. This wasn't my event, it was Robbie's. He's the one we should be congratulating."

Robbie looked pleased, "But I couldn't have done it without you. It was teamwork."

"You're right it was teamwork and the team was far bigger than just you and me. Right, I'll fetch my coat and make a move."

Robbie was still waiting when Gabe returned dressed for the outdoors. As Gabe passed Robbie took his arm and held him in a hug. "Thanks, Gabe. Merry Christmas." And with that, he ran into his flat.

Memoir of an Idiot

Michael came to see me at Harrington Hall today. He liked the Christmas party and watched whilst some of the presents were given out. Everyone seemed to have a whale of a time. There were smiles and laughter throughout the day and everyone helped everyone else. I don't think I've ever had such a lovely day.

Michael says that's me finished now. I have done my community service. Unmapped and unplanned I have passed. I feel torn. I would love to stay and see how Robbie turns out. Or if there is anything between Alison and Sam. Check that the Captain and Miss J are all right. Will Ginny marry Phil? I think he's thinking about asking. And what about Kathy and Jenny? Will Kathy find Mr Right?

I suppose if that's me done there, I need to finish my memoir. I have been an idiot. I know. I can see it. I knew it before I began to write this but writing has made it real. Made it more focused. This final section is far from glamorous.

I used the money from the copper wire job to buy more bags, inevitable. Smike warned me that he had a new supplier so watch how I go. I didn't listen. I was an addict I knew what I was doing. I knew how much I needed.

It was a bright day, early spring. I sat on the bench in a small park. There were a couple throwing sticks for a crazy spaniel, but otherwise, it was solitary. Traffic noise was some distance off. I used the back of my hand to take my dose. The white was greyer and gritty. The fizz in my head was almost instant. The feeling of relaxation, mild euphoria settled over me. I leant back on the seat and closed my eyes. After a while, I felt my body slowly roll to one side but I didn't have the energy to stop it. Somewhere in my head, I realised that I was too tired to breathe. It wasn't a scary awareness. I felt the early sun warming my face, and in my mind, I smiled.

Chapter 60

Boxing Day afternoon Sam knocked on Alison's door and Robbie opened it. "Hi, Robbie. Did you know there's an envelope and present in the lift addressed to you?" Robbie looked surprised. "I noticed it there last night. But I was too whacked to knock then."

Robbie ran to the lift and, as Sam had said there was an envelope with just his name on it, a small package and a large white feather. He lifted the feather and ran it across his face. It was soft and smelt like newly washed clothes, Robbie decided. The ends of the filaments of the feather seemed to have a slight shimmer. He placed it back on the table.

The envelope was pristine and the tag on the back was just tucked in rather than gummed down. Robbie freed it and lifted out a letter. It was large and had been folded to fit inside. He eased it open and flattened it with his hands. He laid it on the table to read.

Dear Robbie,

Thank you for being the boy you are. I've never had a son, but if I had I would have been the proudest dad in the world to have a son like you.

Robbie stopped reading and wiped his eyes. He knew he wasn't going to see Gabe again.

Thank you for agreeing to help me with my Community work and starting the miracle that is The Lift Book Club. I bet nowhere else in the world is there such a thing. It is 100% unique, just as you are. I hope the book club will keep going after I've gone. I think it makes a lot of people really happy.

I'm sorry I had to go without saying goodbye, but it would have been too hard to see you in person and say those words. Coming to Harrington Hall was a second chance for me. I needed to show that I was a good person at heart.

Something I'd lost sight of in recent years. You showed me what it is to be a good person.

Don't think that I don't know some of the things you get up to like the ginger cat last year!

Robbie felt himself blush. He and his best friend, Martin, had tried to persuade a ginger cat to come and live with Robbie. Time and again they brought it to the flat and each time it ran away. Robbie had thought no one else knew about it.

You are not an angel. And hopefully won't be one for a good many years yet! But you are a good person and if nothing else I want you to take that message with you.

The white feather is to remind you that you don't need a 'lucky feather'. You make your own luck with hard work and thoughtfulness. If you haven't opened the little package yet, do that now before you read on.

Robbie took hold of the parcel and unwrapped it. It was only in tissue paper without tape to hold it. Inside was a pair of tiny glass bells with gold decoration. The sort of thing you put on a Christmas tree, Robbie thought. He rattled them and a beautiful chime filled the lift. It reminded Robbie of something.

He took up the letter again.

I thought they could be your Clarence bells. Every time they tinkle on the tree you'll know another angel has got his wings.

Goodbye, Robbie. Give my love to everyone, but keep a large dose for yourself.

Your friend.
Gabe
Xx

Robbie sat in Gabe's chair and lifted the bells. A gentle tinkle was heard.